Princesses of Rydiania

Out of the palace into the limelight!
Three royal sisters, one fairy-tale dream!

When Prince Istvan fell in love and stepped out of
the line of succession, the lives of his three sisters
changed irrevocably.

Princess Gisella became the crown princess,
and her younger sisters, Beatrix and Cecelia,
were expected to step even further into the royal
spotlight and carry the monarchy into the future.

But as they await their brother's royal wedding and
Gisella's coronation, the princesses all begin to
question their place in the palace and discover that
their true hearts' desires might not be exactly as
they imagined...

Read Cecelia and Antoine's story in
His Accidentally Pregnant Princess

And don't miss Beatrix and Rez's story in
Royal Mum for the Duke's Daughter

Both available now!

Watch out for Gisella's story,
coming soon!

D1012476

Dear Reader,

There are times when love silently tiptoes up and startles a couple. When this happens, they sometimes fight the wild rush of emotions. That's what happens with my hero and heroine.

When Rydiania's wedding of the year is in jeopardy, the royal family must pull out all the stops in order to help the bride and groom make it up the aisle. After all, the groom is Princess Beatrix's older brother and she'll do anything to help him— including working with her childhood crush.

Rez Baráth, the Duke of Kaspar, is now a widower and a single father. Wrapped in guilt and overwhelmed with being a single parent, he's spent the past year holed up on his country estate. But Princess Beatrix's urgent phone call changes everything. It draws him from seclusion to the royal palace.

How do you say no to a queen? Hint: you don't. And so when the queen of Rydiania asks the princess and duke to pretend to be a romantic couple in order to distract the paparazzi from the wedding that's in jeopardy, they grudgingly agree to do it. But can a real relationship come from a fake one?

Happy reading,

Jennifer

Royal Mom for the Duke's Daughter

—

Jennifer Faye

Recycling programs
for this product may
not exist in your area.

ISBN-13: 978-1-335-59631-4

Royal Mom for the Duke's Daughter

Copyright © 2023 by Jennifer F. Stroka

For questions and comments about the quality of this book,
please contact us at CustomerService@Harlequin.com.

Harlequin Enterprises ULC
22 Adelaide St. West, 41st Floor
Toronto, Ontario M5H 4E3, Canada
www.Harlequin.com

Printed in U.S.A.

Award-winning author **Jennifer Faye** pens fun contemporary romances. Internationally published with books translated into more than a dozen languages, she is a two-time winner of the *RT Book Reviews* Reviewers' Choice Award and winner of the CataRomance Reviewers' Choice Award. Now living her dream, she resides with her very patient husband and Writer Kitty. When she's not plotting out her next romance, you can find her with a mug of tea and a book. Learn more at jenniferfaye.com.

Books by Jennifer Faye

Harlequin Romance

Princesses of Rydiania

His Accidentally Pregnant Princess

Greek Paradise Escape

Greek Heir to Claim Her Heart
It Started with a Royal Kiss
Second Chance with the Bridesmaid

Wedding Bells at Lake Como

Bound by a Ring and a Secret
Falling for Her Convenient Groom

Fairytale Christmas with the Millionaire

Visit the Author Profile page
at Harlequin.com for more titles.

CHAPTER ONE

ONE FOOT IN front of the other.

It had been Rez Baráth, the Duke of Kaspar's, mantra for the past year. Some days were easier than others. Today was one of the better ones. His fourteen-month-old daughter, Evi, had just taken her first steps.

And though he'd been such a proud papa in the moment, it was when he instinctually thought of telling Enora that her absence from their lives seared through him like a sword straight to his heart. In the past year of grieving his wife's death, he'd started to forget the little details, like the sound of her voice and her contagious laugh.

There were other times when he'd have to pull up a photo of Enora on his phone in order to remember her smile and the way it made her eyes twinkle. Guilt would assail him. How could he let those details grow fuzzy? What was wrong with him?

A moment was all it took for the gravity of

one man's careless action to destroy Rez's perfect family. And now it was up to him to take the jagged pieces of their life and reframe it in order to recreate a family for his daughter.

He could never replace his wife in their daughter's life. Enora was so organized and seemed to instinctively know exactly what their baby daughter needed.

He was quite certain he was making an utter mess of everything. But he refused to give up. He had to keep putting one foot in front of the other and hope he didn't do too much damage.

He was sitting on the floor in the study as the sunlight streamed in through the large windows. Evi was next to him on the floor with her toys. She'd pick up one wooden block, put it to her rosy lips and then toss it aside. It would appear she didn't appreciate the taste of wood.

He'd learned the hard way that it didn't matter how many times he told her not to put things in her mouth, it didn't stop her. Now he just made sure anything within reach was appropriate to be drooled on.

Evi turned her head and smiled at him. He saw his wife in their daughter's smile. His heart swelled with love. Enora would live on through their daughter.

In the next heartbeat, he worried that he

didn't know what was best for Evi. Perhaps he should marry again for Evi's sake. His little girl needed a mother to help guide her in ways he couldn't even imagine. But he just wasn't ready to make such a big commitment.

Instead, he'd immersed himself in his life as a single parent, hoping he could somehow be enough for Evi. He'd even taken a leave of absence from his law firm. But if he didn't return to the office soon, his leave would turn into a resignation.

The funny thing was that when Enora had first mentioned having a family, he hadn't been sure he wanted to be a father. He couldn't envision himself sitting around playing games and doing the middle-of-the-night feedings. And now he couldn't imagine his life without Evi in it. She was the most precious gift that Enora had given him. And he would be eternally grateful that she had known this was right for the both of them.

But he was torn between his responsibilities for Evi and his desire to return to the office. As much as he loved his daughter, he longed for some adult conversation and something to challenge his mind. He had nannies to look after Evi, but with his long hours, he wouldn't see much of Evi. He knew it wasn't what Enora would have wanted for their daughter. Guilt settled on him for wanting to be somewhere else. Because Evi was now the center of his life and she needed him more than ever now that she didn't have a mother.

Buzz-buzz.

It startled him. His phone didn't ring much because he'd pushed most everyone away after his wife's death. The first thing that came to mind was that something was wrong.

When he removed the phone from his pocket, he expected to see his mother's name on the caller ID. But instead it was Princess Beatrix. Why in the world would she want to speak to him?

And then he sighed. How could he have forgotten about the wedding? Her brother's royal wedding. And if his memory was correct, it was in a couple of weeks. He knew he should be more on top of these things since he was the best man. But when Istvan had asked him to stand up for him, Rez had told him that with being a single parent he wasn't the best choice. Istvan had insisted he totally understood. Istvan assured him that he just wanted his childhood best friend there with him on his big day.

Rez pressed the phone to his ear. "What may I do for you, Your Royal Highness?"

"Rez, you know you can just call me Beatrix."

The sound of her gentle voice swept him back in time to a point where they were young and carefree. He missed those days and he found himself missing the Princess too. He highly doubted she'd called to catch-up on life. Although it wouldn't hurt to extend the conversation just a little.

"It's been a while since we really talked and I wasn't sure how you would feel about me taking such liberties. After all, I seem to remember you getting upset with me for calling you—"

"Stop. I remember," she said dryly.

Her seriousness only egged him on. "So then you don't want me to call you Bizzy-Bea?"

"Definitely not." Her voice held no sense of humor. "How about we go with Beatrix?"

Beatrix was almost as bad as Your Highness. It was so proper and the Beatrix he remembered used to be all smiles and giggles. She'd been full of sunshine and rainbows. She'd been the little sister of his best friend and too young for him back then, but he always knew she'd one day grow into a beautiful woman.

But there was a part of him that wanted the

carefree girl of their youth back because he could use some sunshine in his life. "Or Bea."

There was a noted pause on the other end of the phone. He imagined her pursing her lips together as she tapped her foot. The image made him smile—something he didn't do unless in the presence of his daughter.

Bea expelled an exasperated sigh. "Or Beatrix."

It was so good to speak to her. He let out a laugh. He couldn't help it. When had Bizzy-Bea grown up to be so serious? And then he realized it really had been too long since he'd felt the elation of a genuine laugh. When Enora had died, his happiness had been buried with her. Laughter had been sucked into a vacuum and lost in the darkness.

"Rez, the reason I called is because the wedding is in trouble."

"What?" His amusement was long forgotten. "What's going on?"

"You're probably the only person in Rydiania that hasn't read the gossip." When his phone buzzed, she said, "I've sent you the link."

He lowered his phone and put it on speakerphone before he looked at the link. "I don't know why anyone cares what the *Duchess Tales* has to say. They're forever making up nonsense."

"It's more than that this time. Read it."
He clicked on the link and began to read.

Princess-to-Be Banished!

He read the headline again. Beneath the all-caps headline was a photo of Indigo, Istvan's fiancée. Rez was confused. Someone had made a big mistake. Indigo was about to be welcomed into the royal family with open arms.

This royal watcher has some big news for all of you. I have it from an excellent source that Prince Istvan's intended bride is the daughter of a thief, who stole from the crown years ago. The thief, along with his family, was banished not only from the royal court but also from the entire country of Rydiania.

You've heard it here first. This duchess has sworn to keep you up on the latest with the royal family and I am doing just that.

You might ask how something like this could have happened. Well, you aren't alone. I assure you, I am hard at work on securing the nitty-gritty details on how this fiasco could have happened.

Did Indigo deceive our lusciously handsome prince? Or was the Prince hoping to carry off this illegal affair in public, hoping us royal watchers wouldn't catch on?

Surely poor Prince Istvan has been duped by the conniving princess-to-be, who wasn't even supposed to be in this country. Did she really think that by using her mother's maiden name she would get away with this level of deception?

Keep reading, my lovely watchers, as I will share the details as they unfold.

This was outrageous! Preposterous. And perhaps a bit worrisome.

"The palace should go after the Duchess for slander and defamation." Anger pulsed through his veins. "The case should be announced loud and clear as a warning so no one else tries the same thing."

"I don't know. It would be up to the King and Queen. Anyway I need, erm… We need you to come and stay at the palace. I think it's going to take all of us to keep this wedding on track."

The palace was a few hours south of his country estate. It was too far for him to conveniently commute back and forth with the hope of spending quality time with Evi. If he was to help, he'd need to stay at the palace. He hadn't left his home since his wife died.

And yet he felt compelled by the great debt he owed Istvan.

He took the phone off speaker and pressed it to his ear. "You really think me coming there will help?"

"I do. You didn't see Indigo's face when she first saw those headlines. She was utterly crushed. And you know how much my parents hate scandal."

Was he ready to reenter society? His presence at the palace would be exactly that. There would be paparazzi lurking at the gate keeping track of the comings and goings of palace guests. The thought of dealing with the press knotted up his gut.

He never left his estate these days. He stayed at home with his daughter, but he was also deeply indebted to the Prince. If it wasn't for Istvan, he wouldn't even have his little girl. The Prince had saved his baby daughter's life.

He owed his best friend more than he could ever repay. He owed him his life because if anything had happened to Evi… He drew his thoughts up short. He refused to imagine a life without his sweet, adorable Evi in it. It was tortuous enough having lost his wife.

He'd never forget what his friend had done risking his own life. And that was why he was still here having this conversation with Bea.

A conversation he didn't want to have. But a debt he was driven to repay. He'd sworn if Istvan ever needed him, he would be there for him—even if the repayment ended up being a steep one.

It was with the greatest hesitation that he said, "I'll come, but I need to bring Evi and her nanny. I can't be away from my daughter for any great length of time."

"I understand. Please bring them."

"All right. I'll be there tomorrow."

"Couldn't you come sooner?" There was a note of desperation in her voice.

"As in today?"

"Oh, yes. That would be perfect. Thank you." She ended the call.

He couldn't believe Bea had convinced him to go to the palace. He had no idea how he could help the situation. He supposed he could lend a shoulder for Istvan to lean on.

Still, going to the palace, where he would have to be sociable. He didn't do social these days. Perhaps remaining within the palace walls and away from the press wouldn't be so bad. It was for his best friend, who would do the same for him.

CHAPTER TWO

THE PALACE WAS ABUZZ.

And not in a good way.

The bride and groom were at odds. Beatrix wanted to help them, but she didn't know what she could do to rectify this awful situation. She was used to being the peacemaker in the family, but she was out of her element when the threat came from outside the palace walls.

At the moment, she was the only bridesmaid in Rydiania. The other two bridesmaids were in Greece on a little resort island called Ludus. It's where Indigo used to work. As for the groomsmen, Istvan had picked three of his childhood friends. One was out of the country until the eve of the wedding. Another was with his wife who was due to give birth to their first child any day now. So that left her and Rez to do what they could to help Istvan and Indigo. But how?

Her thoughts turned to the Queen. Her mother was the one who protected the family and the royal name. Her mother had dedicated her life to doing whatever was necessary to protect the royal family. It used to bother Beatrix the way her mother would manipulate people and circumstances to make the palace shine, but perhaps in this particular instance her mother's skills were exactly what they needed. She worried that even the Queen might not be wily enough to right what had gone so drastically wrong.

Indigo had just called off the wedding before fleeing the palace with Istvan in pursuit. Beatrix hoped they were able to work things out. If it wasn't for that gossip site, they'd still be happily preparing for their wedding.

Beatrix rushed down the grand staircase to update the Queen on the bride and groom's departure, but before she reached the bottom step, Rez walked in the door. She came to an immediate halt a few steps from the bottom. The breath caught in her lungs. Rez grew increasingly handsome with every passing year.

When she was a teenager, she'd had the biggest crush on him. Of course, he'd been five years older than her and her older brother's best friend. Rez had never looked at her as anything but a little sister. Looking back on those times, she was mortified at the way she'd mooned over him.

Ever since he'd announced his engagement, she'd kept her distance from him, lest her brother tease her for her childhood crush. Why did her brother have to have a memory like an elephant?

Rez was tall, even taller than Istvan. He was certainly a man to be reckoned with, but as she recalled he didn't have a temper unless provoked. Otherwise he'd been easygoing and fun to be around.

He was also the most delicious eye candy. Rez's broad shoulders filled out the dark suit he was wearing. He had certainly bulked up since they were kids. She hadn't allowed herself to notice in the past, but now, well, he was a widower. Not that she had any intention of starting anything with him.

His dark hair was longer than he normally wore it. She'd guess he didn't get his hair trimmed all that often now that he was still spending all of his time holed up on his estate. Even though she made a point not to go out of her way to be informed about his life, it was impossible not to hear the gossip. From what she'd heard he'd all but given up on life after the tragic death of his young wife. But it was his baby daughter that kept him going.

Beatrix's heart went out to him. She couldn't even imagine all he'd gone through and now to be a single parent. She couldn't imagine what it must be like to start off co-parenting only to wake up one day and be doing it all alone. It must be quite a shock.

Her gaze met his piercing blue gaze. Her heart leaped to her throat. Had he caught her checking him out? She hoped not. If so, it would make for a very awkward start to things.

In a much slower pace, she continued down the last step to the marble floor. As she neared him, she considered giving him a brief hug and feathery kiss like old friends were prone to do. But the rigid line of his shoulders and the frown on his handsome face had her maintaining her distance.

She hoped when she spoke that her voice would sound normal. "Rez, thank you for coming."

He didn't say anything for a moment. "It's been a while since we've seen each other. You're still as beautiful as ever."

Heat bloomed in her chest and rushed to her cheeks. "Thank you. You're looking good too." Her heart pitter-pattered. She licked her dry lips. "I just wish you were here under different circumstances."

"I do too. I take it things haven't improved."

Beatrix shook her head. "It's a mess." She glanced around. "Did Evi come with you?"

"The nanny has taken her upstairs." He hesitated. "Would you like to meet her?"

Beatrix found herself caught off guard by the change in Rez's demeanor. "Perhaps it would be best to let her get settled. She must be tired after the car ride."

"Actually she slept most of the way." His eyes were guarded. "And she'd like to meet you."

Beatrix worried that he was going to continue pushing the subject of meeting his daughter. She noticed how the frown disappeared from his face whenever he mentioned his daughter. Beatrix was happy he had that special relationship.

She sometimes wondered if she would have been a good parent. As soon as the thought came to her, she pushed it away. There was no point pondering something that wasn't going to happen. It broke her heart when the doctor had told her that between the severity of her endometriosis and the surgeries that she'd never be able to carry a baby of her own.

But she'd dealt with the devastating news and made peace with her life without children. Unlike her brother and sister, she knew her life was going to be one of service. She liked— no, she loved being out among the people and shining a light on areas of life that needed assistance.

Luckily she wasn't the heir apparent—that had been her brother, Prince Istvan. However, with him stepping out of line for the crown, her older sister, Gisella, was now the Crown Princess. And so it didn't matter to the palace if Beatrix had children or not.

But seeing Rez again was bringing back all of her youthful dreams of creating a life with him—a life that had included children to carry on his lineage. Children that would resemble their handsome father.

And suddenly it was like she'd just learned the news once more that she couldn't carry a baby of her own. She felt the loss profoundly. Tears pricked the backs of her eyes. She blinked them away. A fundamental choice that had been taken from her.

"Come." Rez gestured for her to follow him. "I'll introduce you to Evi."

Beatrix didn't move. Her heart clutched in her chest. She wasn't ready for this, especially not with the man whose babies she'd once dreamed of having and now that could never be.

Rez stopped at the bottom of the steps and turned back, but before either of them could speak one of the Queen's footmen in all of his black and purple finery appeared.

He bowed. "Your Royal Highness, the Queen has requested your presence in her office." The young man turned to Rez. "The Queen has requested your attendance as well."

Beatrix expelled a gentle sigh of relief. As they started in the direction of the Queen's office, she couldn't help but feel she'd dodged a bullet.

She glanced over at Rez. But how long could she make excuses not to meet Evi before Rez suspected something? She wasn't prepared to see his sweet baby girl. It would drive home exactly what she was going to miss in life.

She worried that she wouldn't be able to keep her emotions under control. He'd push until she confessed the painful truth. And she wasn't ready to share with him that she couldn't have children. The only people that knew were her immediate family. And that's how she intended to keep it.

CHAPTER THREE

"THANK YOU FOR COMING." The Queen sat behind her large oak desk.

Beatrix couldn't help but notice the stress lines marring her mother's face making her look much older. Her mother usually took things in stride but things within the palace walls had been tumultuous lately. This latest scandal was taking a toll on everyone.

Beatrix wondered if she'd done the right thing by asking Rez to come to the palace. She hadn't thought through her plan before extending the invitation. Of course he'd want to bring his daughter. Now she worried that her emotions over her diagnosis might not be as resolved as she'd thought they were.

Just then the door opened behind her. Beatrix turned to find her sister Gisella, followed by the King. The King's eyes momentarily widened when he saw everyone congregating in the Queen's office.

Once the door was closed, all eyes turned toward the Queen, who turned to Beatrix. "You have news?"

"I do." Beatrix filled them in on the big fight between Istvan and Indigo. "And now Indigo has left the Kingdom. I think if we're going to help them we need to know the story behind the headline."

The King moved to stand next to the Queen. "It's a story we were hoping to keep under wraps because it's so painful for Indigo."

"But that's impossible now," the Queen said. "It's just a matter of time until the press knows all of the details. If only Istvan had fallen in love with someone else, the most painful page in this family's history wouldn't have to be revisited."

"This has something to do with Uncle Georgios?" Beatrix asked.

The King nodded. "Indigo's father was King Georgios's private secretary. When your uncle left Rydiania, so did his personal staff."

"You exiled his staff too?" This was the first Beatrix was hearing of this. She'd been very young when this had all happened so she had no memories of it.

"It had to be done," the Queen said. "All precautions had to be taken to ensure the future of the crown. We couldn't have powerful people with connections as well as an absolute allegiance to Georgios causing problems. After all, your father wasn't asked to step into this role. It had been thrust upon us when Georgios decided being king was too much for him and went to live on that Greek island."

"But that never included Indigo or her mother," the King said. "Now we have to hope Istvan will be able to make Indigo realize that the royal family will support her through this trying time."

"What are we going to do now?" Beatrix asked.

"Do?" Gisella looked at her. "There's nothing to do. Indigo chose to leave. We have to hope Istvan can get through to her."

Beatrix shook her head. "Not about that. We need to keep the news of Indigo calling off the wedding and leaving the country from the paparazzi."

"I agree," the Queen said. "And with blood in the water, so to speak, the press is going to be all over this latest development."

"Hopefully Istvan can convince her to come back right away," Gisella said. "That should put to rest any rumors of the wedding being in jeopardy."

"I wish that was the case," Beatrix said, "but you didn't see Indigo when she left here. I don't think she'll be back anytime soon."

The Queen turned to the King with narrowed brows and her lips pursed. "I told you we needed to deal with her past from the start, but you caved in to her wants and thought it could all be buried."

He frowned. "Now isn't the time for throwing around the blame. What we need is a plan. And since you're so good at them, what do you suggest?"

The Queen looked directly at Beatrix. "We need a story that will tease away the press from the wedding."

The family threw around some ideas. While they talked, Beatrix glanced over at Rez. He was absolutely silent. By his blank expression, she was unable to read what he was thinking. She remembered that particular look from when they were kids. It had helped him feign innocence from childhood pranks.

But all of these years later there was something different about him. It was the pain that would periodically glimmer in his eyes when he didn't think anyone was looking. It had been more than a year since he'd lost his wife and his pain was still tangible. She wished there was something she could do to comfort him.

Just then Rez turned his head enough for his gaze to meet hers. She was busted. Heat swirled in her chest, rushed up her neck and settled in her cheeks. For a second, their gazes locked. Then the corners of his mouth started to lift as his eyes twinkled with amusement. Was he laughing at her?

With a soft huff, she turned away. What had she been thinking to get busted staring at him? And it wasn't like she'd been ogling him because she was interested in him. She'd gotten over her childhood crush many years ago. Luckily no one else seemed to have noticed their silent exchange.

"What can we do to help?" Gisella asked, drawing Beatrix from her thoughts.

"Obviously no one can mention that Indigo and Istvan have left the palace," the King said. "We're going to imply that they are here working on some final wedding details."

"Mother," Beatrix said, "you mentioned something about distracting the press. Do you have a suggestion of how we could go about doing that?"

"What about a new romance?" the Queen suggested.

Everyone wore a look of surprise. There were a bunch of shrugs. The only problem was that none of them were in a relationship or even on the verge of one.

"Don't look at me," Gisella said. "I've got

enough going on with the upcoming coronation."

"Of course, dear," the Queen said. "And we wouldn't want our soon-to-be queen involved in a fake relationship."

All of the sudden everyone turned in Beatrix's direction. Her spine stiffened. *Oh, no. No, no, no.* Surely they didn't think she was going to pretend to be in a relationship. Who was going to buy that? Everyone knew she hadn't dated anyone in the past year. And she wasn't planning to start now.

Ever since the last man she'd been involved with had proposed, she realized letting herself get that close to anyone was a mistake. She wasn't ready to be married. And there was the complication of her not being able to have a family of her own that would have to be addressed before any wedding proposal could seriously be considered.

When she'd put off her ex's marriage proposal, it had gone horribly wrong. Before she could explain to him about her infertility issues, he'd accused her of being fickle—of not knowing what she wanted. After his tirade, she'd ended things altogether. Ever since then she'd been hesitant to get seriously involved with anyone.

Her life was full with royal obligations and

her pet projects. Her spare time was spent on the golf course. She loved the game, the sunshine and the challenge of beating some of the finest golfers in Europe. Did she really need anything more?

And yet it was so natural for her to step up when her family needed help. After all, she had devoted her life to one of service. But this seemed above and beyond the call of duty.

Beatrix swallowed hard. "No one is going to believe it's me. Everyone knows I'm taking a break from dating."

The Queen's eyes lit up. "That's all the more reason it'll draw the paparazzi's interest."

Beatrix shook her head. "I don't think so. There has to be another way."

As though Beatrix hadn't said a word, the Queen continued. "All we need is someone to play your love interest."

It didn't seem to matter what she said, her mother was already set on this course of action. And as much as Beatrix wanted to help her brother and Indigo, this just seemed like a bad idea.

Beatrix watched as her family turned to Rez. She gaped. Not him. Definitely not him.

She snapped her mouth closed. Her heart raced as her breathing came in short, shallow gasps. She lowered her head and stared at the floor, hoping her family wouldn't notice that she was on the verge of a full-blown panic attack.

This couldn't be happening. Of all the people in the Kingdom, why did it have to be him? She refused to look in Rez's direction. The thought of them pretending to be a couple caused the heat to return to her cheeks. She struggled to get a hold on her panicked emotions and she was failing badly.

She concentrated on slowing her breaths by breathing in, holding her breath and then slowly expelling it. Surely Rez wouldn't agree to any of this. She took some comfort in the thought. Her racing heart rate began to slow. After all, he was still grieving for his wife. There was no way he'd want to get involved in a scheme like this.

"What do you say, Rez?" the King asked.

That wasn't fair. Who was going to turn down a direct request from the King? Beatrix's back teeth clenched as she bit back her frustration. For a moment, an awkward silence ensued.

"Are we sure this is the direction we want to go?" Rez asked very diplomatically.

The King arched a brow. "Do you have a better idea?"

Rez was quiet for a moment as though he

was scrambling for a different idea. "No, sir. I just worry that the press will see through the charade."

"They won't question you two getting together. It's well-known that you grew up together. I think the public will be elated with the idea of you two dating." The Queen's direct gaze met his. "Do you feel this is something you could do to help the Prince?"

There was a distinct hesitation.

Beatrix lifted her gaze. Why wasn't he turning down the preposterous proposal? What was he waiting for? Maybe he was stunned into silence. Yes, that must be it.

"Yes, ma'am." His answer reverberated in Beatrix's mind.

No, no, no. What was he doing?

"Good. Now that it's settled," the Queen said, "my staff will work on a series of appearances for Rez and Beatrix." When Beatrix went to voice her displeasure with this arrangement, the Queen was quick to add, "Prince Istvan will be indebted to you both."

Beatrix considered doing something she'd never done as an adult by refusing the Queen's request. Although if she were to do that the King would step in and demand she do as she was told. It would also mean the Queen would take a more active role in this subterfuge. At least this way, the Queen was leaving the details up to her and Rez to work out.

As if on cue, the Queen's secretary was bid entrance to the office. She spoke softly in the Queen's ear. The Queen turned back to everyone. "I'm sorry but I must attend to another matter."

Both the King and Queen exited the office, leaving Beatrix facing her smiling sister. Beatrix inwardly groaned. Whatever Gisella had to say was best said in private—far away from Rez.

"Gisella, can you excuse us?" She implored her sister with her eyes to leave her alone with Rez.

"Just let me know if you two lovebirds need me." Gisella laughed as she walked away.

Once the door closed behind her sister, Beatrix turned to Rez. "Why do you want to do this?"

"I don't recall me ever saying I wanted to do this. Why didn't you tell your mother no?"

She reached for the first reason she could find. "Because there's protocol to follow. And you don't say no to a direct request from the Queen."

He arched a disbelieving brow. "I can't believe you follow protocol."

She frowned at him. "What's that supposed to mean?"

"It's just that I remember you as a kid speaking up and not worrying about protocol."

When she was little she did speak her mind, but what he didn't realize was that she spoke up when there was a problem within the family to resolve. She never liked to hear people she cared about in an argument. Her two sisters would argue all of the time. Gisella was the rule-follower and Cecelia was the rule-breaker. It caused a lot of distress in the family.

It was pointed out to her more than once that she was good at dealing with people. At first, she didn't believe it. As she grew older, she realized that she could talk to most anyone. And that's when she decided to dedicate her life to one of service. She loved people and wanted to help them to the best of her ability.

"That was a long time ago." Just like her crush on him was a long time ago. "If you haven't noticed, I'm not a kid any longer." But she was still a nurturer, even at her own expense.

"I've noticed."

She wasn't sure what to make of his comment. Was it just a matter of fact? Or was he implying something?

CHAPTER FOUR

HE COULDN'T BELIEVE this was happening.

Rez wasn't happy that the Queen had maneuvered him into faking a relationship with Princess Beatrix. It was the very last thing he wanted to do.

He should have never left his country estate. It was there where he could close himself off from the rest of the world. Behind closed doors, he didn't have to face the public's pitying looks or have well-meaning busybodies try to set him up on a blind date.

At home is where he should be—it's where he belonged. Not here. Not embarking upon a fake romantic relationship.

He raked his fingers through his short hair, not caring if he messed it up. "You're right. I shouldn't have agreed. I've got to go."

"Go where?"

"Home. I'm not the right person for this plan." He turned and headed toward the door.

Bea rushed around him. She stopped in

front of the closed doors and pressed her hands to her curvy hips. For the first time, he really noticed how his best friend's little sister had grown up in all the right places. He swallowed hard.

"You can't go now," she said as a matter of fact.

"Of course I can."

"But you told the Queen you would do this."

"I never told her I would do it. I said I could do it… If I wanted to." He saw the worried look on her face. "Don't worry. I'm sure there's a long line of guys that would be willing to stand in as your boyfriend."

"It can't just be anyone." Her brows drew together. "Don't you understand? It has to be someone who cares deeply about Istvan and Indigo. Someone willing to do what it takes to protect their happiness."

"I understand. I'm sorry. It can't be me."

The disappointment showed on her face. She stepped aside. "I understand." Sympathy shone in her eyes. "I got so caught up in the drama that I didn't think about how hard this would be for you."

His gut knotted up. He couldn't deal with her pity. "I'm fine."

She arched a disbelieving brow. "I don't think you are."

"I said I am." His words came out with more force than he'd intended. "You know when you asked me to come here, I was only intending to comfort an old friend and give him a shoulder to lean on. I didn't expect," he waved his arms around, "all of this."

"What can I say? The Queen takes matters into her own hands and sometimes the solutions are rather elaborate."

"Surely there has to be another solution." He began to pace.

"We had everyone in the room and no one came up with a better idea." She looked at him. "Unless you have something you failed to mention to my parents."

He stopped pacing. "If I did, I would have mentioned it before."

Her hopes were quickly dashed. But she had to admit that her mother was right about one thing, the press loved a royal secret. If the fans could ferret out a secret via the press, it would be all the rage. And maybe there's a way they could use that to their advantage.

"I have an idea," Beatrix said.

He turned to her, pressed his hands to his sides and frowned. "Am I going to like it?"

"I don't think so but it's at least better than what my mother is proposing." She gestured for him to follow her. "Let's go out in the garden. It's too gloomy in here."

There was a moment or two when he didn't move, but eventually she heard him sigh. Soon after his footsteps sounded behind her. She led them out the back door, across the expansive terrace, down the steps and along the garden path.

By now Rez was beside her. "Where are we going?"

"For a walk. It's such a beautiful day and I thought the sunshine might cheer you up."

"I don't need any cheering up." His words were clipped and gruff.

She turned to him and smiled. "Am I supposed to believe you?"

He sighed again as he stopped walking. "I don't have time for a stroll in the garden. I have things to do."

"What things do you do?" She meant it honestly. She didn't know anything about Rez's life since he left court to go have a quiet life with his wife and daughter at his country estate.

"Things. You know." He glanced down at the gravel as he shifted his weight from one foot to the other. "And Evi needs me."

It sounded to her like he was making excuses to leave. And that couldn't happen because as much as she hated her mother's idea, it was the only distraction that would have a chance to distract the paparazzi.

She began walking again. Rez was either going to join her or he was going to turn around and return to his estate.

"Would you stop walking?" His footfalls crunched over the gravel. "Just talk to me."

She ignored his grumping and let the warm rays of the sun ease the tension in her shoulders. She didn't stop until she was out of sight of the palace. The time gave her a chance to polish up her idea. She didn't have all of the ins and outs worked out but it was getting there.

Rez glanced around. "Now that we're alone, would you mind telling me your plan? And will it get us out of this fake dating?"

"Not exactly." This time she was the one to stop walking. She turned to him. "If we just date, it'll be one headline on the tabloid sites."

"What are you suggesting?"

"That we sneak around."

He shook his head. "This is sounding more involved instead of making things easier."

"No. Think about it. We won't have to really date."

"I'm confused. Are we going to have a fake relationship or not?"

"We are. But it has to be a cat-and-mouse sort of game with the press. A look here. A touch there. Just enough to get people wondering and talking. Because if they are talking about us, they won't be noticing that Istvan and Indigo aren't here."

Rez didn't look convinced. In fact, he looked as though he was ready to bolt. How in the world was she going to convince him that this idea could actually work?

The press had taken notice of her single status. In fact, someone let it leak that she'd sworn off men for a year. So for her to break her one-year pledge of no dating after only ten months, well, it would be noted by the press.

And as awful as it might sound, a widower—a single father—entering the dating scene would be big news, especially since it had crushed a lot of hearts when Rez had married. Together, they were bound to make headline news on all of the gossip sites— especially the *Duchess Tales*.

Why was he still here?

Rez should have turned around and left as soon as he learned Istvan had departed to go after Indigo. Why hadn't he done just that? The answer instantly came to him. Bea.

Once he saw her, he'd wanted to stick around. He wanted to talk to her—to get to know her again. After he'd married, he lost contact with most of the people at court. It was like he'd stopped being one person and become another—a husband and a father.

And then he'd started to take his life for granted. He thought that Enora would always be there and Bea would always be off-limits to him. He'd never been so wrong in his life.

While Bea had been cute as a kid with her long braids that he would occasionally tug on and the innocent joy that would light up her face, as a woman she was gorgeous with her blue eyes that felt as though they could see into the deepest, darkest corners of his soul to her curvy figure that teased and taunted his imagination.

The fact he saw her that way wasn't good. Not good at all. He didn't want to be attracted to her. It wasn't right when Enora's memory was still with him.

The best thing he could do was to turn around and head home. Because pretending to be involved with Bea would be like playing with matches. One wrong move and they'd both go up in hot, burning flames of desire.

He couldn't allow that to happen. He didn't deserve to be happy again. He'd made a bunch of wrong choices and in the end, he'd lost his wife. If only he could go back in time, he would make other choices and Evi would still have her mother. It's what he wished for each night—just another chance for a do-over.

And yet the debt he owed Istvan kept him from moving. If this is what it took to help, he would do it—even if he didn't like it.

"What exactly are you suggesting?" he asked.

"That we start appearing in the same places."

"Together?"

She frowned at him. "Weren't you listening? We have to play this stealthily."

He once more raked his fingers through his hair, scattering the short strands. "And when do you want to start?"

"Right away." She paused.

"What does that mean?"

"I'm trying to think of an event for this evening, but I can't recall one. But tomorrow there's a polo match. I can go with some friends. Do you have someone you can show up with?"

Did she think he was that pathetic that he didn't have any friends? He might have holed up in his home after his wife's death for a while—for the past year, but he still had friends—even if he hadn't talked to them in a long time.

"Of course." He could call some of the guys he and Istvan palled around with. And then a better idea came to him. "What if I were to play?"

"Polo?"

"Yes." It'd been a year since he'd played but he hadn't forgotten any of it. And his team had said when he was ready to return that they would have him back.

"Do you think that's a good idea? You know. After you've been away from it for so long."

"I guess we'll find out." The more he thought about it, the more anxious he became to be back in the game.

In that moment, he realized just how much he'd withdrawn from life while he'd tried being father and mother to his little girl. The problem was that he could never be a mother to Evi. His daughter deserved a loving and devoted mother, not his attempts at being something he was not.

"Rez, did you hear me?" Bea sent him a worried look.

He had absolutely no idea what she'd said. "Of course I did."

"Good. So you'll call your friends while I work on other social engagements."

"How exactly will this work?"

"Well, for starters an anonymous source will leak to the *Duchess Tales* that you have reentered society."

He wasn't so sure how he felt about that. There was a part of him that felt guilty that he could just go on with his life while his wife's had been cut so very short. "And then?"

"Then you and I will make an appearance at the polo match. Maybe you could think about playing. Anyway I'll be excited to see you."

"And that's it? It doesn't seem very headline-worthy."

"True. Maybe we'll hug. Would that be better?"

With all of her curvy goodness, it definitely wouldn't be better. Because he was quickly finding the more he was around her, the less he thought clearly.

He swallowed hard. "It's at least something."

"We can't give them too much or else they won't be interested. We'll be a one-off headline and they won't follow us around. Remember we have to get them off the scent of Indigo and Istvan."

"Don't you ever get tired of dealing with the paparazzi?" He didn't know how she lived with it day in and day out. While he'd been at his country estate, no one had bothered with him and that's the way he liked it.

"Of course. Who wouldn't? But in this case, they will be helpful." She smiled as though proud of herself for outsmarting the press. "Anyway, after we hug and chat a little, I'll go off with my friends and you'll go with yours to watch the match."

"And that's it?" He should be able to do this. It didn't sound too terribly bad.

"Yes. At least for tomorrow. I have to check the social calendar and find out what options we have for the following day."

"So this is going to be an everyday occurrence?"

"Yes, until Istvan and Indigo return. Now we should head inside. We have arrangements to make." She turned and headed back toward the palace. When he didn't walk with her, she stopped and turned. "Aren't you coming?"

"In a moment. You go on ahead."

She nodded and continued on her way.

He needed a moment to gather his thoughts. He'd come here thinking he'd have to lend moral support to his oldest friend. Instead his friend had flown off to Greece chasing after his bride and now Rez was left dealing with his best friend's little sister—the sister who had a blatant crush on him when they were kids.

Istvan had emphatically warned him off his sister. Not that Rez would have ever made a move on Bea with her being a few years younger than him.

The problem now was with their ages no longer an issue, temptation had reared its annoying head. And as cute as Bea had been as a kid, she had blossomed into the most enticing woman. Not that he was looking for anyone to get involved with—far from it. But it didn't diminish his desire to hold her in his arms.

CHAPTER FIVE

AND SO THE royal charade was in motion.

It even had the King and Queen's blessing.

Beatrix couldn't help but be surprised that her mother had proposed this outrageous plan. Sure, the Queen could be quite cunning when necessary, but her plans didn't usually involve using her own children as decoys. This just drove home how concerned the King and Queen must be about Istvan's future and that of the royal family.

Scandals took their tolls on the Kingdom and could last decades or even centuries. To this day, her parents were still dealing with the fallout of her uncle's abdication. Ever since that monumental day, the royal family had been under the scrutiny of the press. Thankfully her mother and father were naturals at filling the position of king and queen. The people of the Kingdom loved them, but everyone was aware of how quickly public opinion could change.

Her parents were very social. They hosted foreign dignitaries at the palace on a regular basis, which was good for Rydiania's economy. The press seemed pleased with their work, until her father had been diagnosed with Parkinson's disease. And now it was time for him to slow down and take care of his health. It was the first bit of news since her uncle's abdication to rock the Kingdom.

Luckily the Kingdom loved her older brother, Istvan. And no one batted an eye at the thought of him stepping up to take over the throne. However, her brother had his own passions, including a foundation for sick children and their families. The Kingdom's charter would have forced Istvan to step away from that very important work in order to become king. And so by rejecting his birthright in order to marry the love of his life, he would still be able to do very important work for the Kingdom. That was if the wedding still took place.

Beatrix wanted to speak to her brother and see how things were going, but now wasn't the time. Beatrix and two of her friends had just arrived at the polo match. She'd known Jolan and Mari since they were kids. They were her closest friends.

As they walked toward the seating area,

Beatrix focused on everything she was supposed to do that day. Because this public appearance was not one of leisure, as the Queen had been quick to remind her at breakfast.

The thought of rushing along her fake relationship with Rez was utmost in her mind. The faster it went, the sooner it'd be over. And the less risk of her getting caught up in the feelings she'd had for him all of those years ago.

But she realized that hurrying along the fake relationship was the exact wrong thing to do. She inwardly groaned. A slower approach to their romance would draw more attention—have more spies watching their every move. And then the focus would be off her brother and his intended bride, giving them time to sort things out.

Today her duty was to "accidentally" run into Rez. They were keeping it under wraps that he was staying at the palace for at least a few more days to give his public appearances more of a buzz.

"Why are you so quiet?" Mari asked.

"Yeah, you don't look happy to be here." Jolan moved to Beatrix's other side. "If you want we can set you up with someone. We know how you need some help in that department." They both laughed at their joke because Beatrix was never short on dates.

Beatrix frowned. "You two are *not* funny."

"Oh, lighten up," Jolan said. "You know that you could have your pick of dates."

"But she doesn't want to," Mari said in support. "She's what…ten months into her year-long break from dating?"

"Yes." Beatrix nodded. "And I like it so much that I might make it two years."

"Two years?" her friends said in unison.

"I don't know why everyone is so worried about my dating life. It isn't like I'm planning to get married…at least not anytime soon."

Jolan sighed. "You know that everything your family does is headline news."

"How could I forget?" she muttered, thinking of the malicious headlines about Indigo. "Enough about me."

It was a beautiful sunny day. Thankfully women were expected to wear hats at the games. Beatrix wore a white woven hat with a yellow ribbon and a wide brim with a mesh band around the edge.

It matched her white top with a short yellow skirt. Her only problem was trying to walk in heels outdoors because she didn't like the way flats looked on her. And since she fully expected to be photographed today, she wanted to look her best.

"Oh, look, isn't that Vera and Niki?" Mari pointed to a group of people off in the distance.

"It is them. I've been trying to get a hold of Niki all week," Jolan said. "Let's go talk to them."

Beatrix wasn't ready to talk to people just yet. "You guys go ahead. I'll catch up with you later."

Her insides shivered with nerves. What if she wasn't any good at feigning surprise? What if no one noticed her with Rez? Although they had planned to meet in front of the viewing area.

Every part of this afternoon had been planned down to the finest detail. They even had a member of the palace staff calling in an anonymous tip that Rez would be attending the polo match today. Now that he was a widower and a year had passed since he lost his wife, he was once again one of the most eligible bachelors in Europe. She wondered how he felt about that title considering his circumstances.

She moved toward the edge of the field. She watched as the ponies and players moved about the field before the game. Her gaze sought out Rez. He was going to be an alternate today as a defender.

It took her a moment to find him, but at last she spotted him atop his mount. He was wearing the number three. As though he spotted her at exactly the same time, he guided his horse toward her.

A smile lifted the corners of her lips. He dismounted and approached her. He didn't smile back. In fact, he looked stressed. She was going to have to work hard to make this impromptu meeting look like a happy reunion.

"Rez, it's so good to see you." She brightened her smile, hoping he would follow suit.

He stood there stiff and unmoving. This wasn't good. Hoping to salvage the situation, she leaned forward to give him a quick hug and a feathery kiss.

To her surprise, his arm wrapped around her and held her close. Her heart pitter-pattered. For a moment, she forgot this was all for show. She forgot they were in public. She forgot they had an audience.

All she could think about was how much she enjoyed being so close to him. It would be so easy to get used to this familiarity. In that moment, she wanted him to be the Rez she remembered—quiet, thoughtful and with a gentle sense of humor. She wondered if she'd ever see that version of him again.

In her ear he whispered, "I don't know what I'm supposed to do."

She felt sorry for him. At the same time, she felt guilty for letting herself enjoy the moment. It wasn't easy to perform in front of an audience. Lucky for her, she had a lifetime of experience.

"Just smile and say something funny." She inhaled his spicy cologne mixed with the earthy scent of the barn. He smelled good. Perhaps too good.

"I'm not funny."

"You have to let me go."

"Oh, right." His arm released her.

She pulled back and immediately missed the feel of his touch. Out of the corner of her eye, she noticed people glancing in their direction. It was time to put on a good show.

She glanced to the side. A photographer had captured their moment together. Mission accomplished. She should feel good that all was going according to plan, but she was worried about Rez. This was so much more difficult for him than she'd imagined.

As she stared at the photographer, he snapped another picture. It was too late to change paths now. She would just have to help

Rez any way she could think of. The game was on.

"It's so good to see you." Her gaze met his.

In a low voice, he said, "You knew I'd be here."

She let out a laugh like he'd said something really funny. Boy was he nervous. It looked like she was on her own to make this look like a fun run-in. "Rez, you forget that we're playacting. Please smile and look like you're happy to see me."

"I wish I was anywhere but here." And then he forced a barely there smile.

"There, that wasn't so bad, was it?"

When his smile broadened, it made her heart pitter-patter. Maybe this situation wasn't going to be as stressful as she'd originally imagined. Perhaps Rez realized their time together didn't have to be miserable. After all, once upon a time they had been friends—perhaps even good friends.

It was then that she noticed he wasn't looking at her. His gaze was focused over her shoulder. So if he wasn't smiling at her, whom was he smiling at?

She turned, expecting to find some beautiful young woman, but there was no one behind her. Her gaze continued searching until her gaze stumbled across a pink baby stroller.

She turned back to him. "Is Evi here?"

The smile fell from his face as he turned his attention back to her. "She is. When I spoke to some of the guys on the team, they insisted I bring her. And her nanny was eager for some sunshine."

Beatrix hadn't expected Evi to be at the game. It was so sweet that he wanted his little girl close by. The love he had for Evi was glaringly evident. She wondered what it was like to have a love so great.

"It sounds like you made the most of the day."

"Come meet her. You didn't get a chance yesterday."

Her heart stuttered. Could she do this? Up until her endometriosis diagnosis, she hadn't given much thought to having a family of her own. After all, she'd been young, marriage and babies weren't on her mind. She'd been focused on forging her own path in life and traveling.

And then in one day—one visit to the doctor—she found herself not able to have something other women took for granted—a baby of her own. At the time, she'd told herself it was no big deal, but now she realized she'd been lying to herself.

Rez stared expectantly at her, making her

heart race and her palms to grow damp. She had to say something—but what? Was she ready to hold Rez's baby in her arms all the while knowing she could never have a baby of her own? And if she couldn't do this, how did she explain it to him?

"Bea?" His voice drew her from her thoughts.

Her palms grew damp. She wasn't ready for this. Not yet.

Her gaze searched the area, looking for an excuse to get out of meeting his daughter. Her focus latched on to her two friends off in the distance. They were headed in her direction.

"Maybe later," she said. "I promised Jolan and Mari that I'd meet up with them."

A distinct frown appeared on his face as her friends rushed up to her. Beatrix braced herself for the onslaught of questions because her friends knew she'd had the biggest crush on Rez in school. They used to pick on her mercilessly.

Without a word, Rez mounted his polo pony. He took off before her friends reached her side.

Mari's eyes lit up. "What were you and Rez talking about?"

"What's he doing here?" Jolan asked. "I didn't think he ever went out in public after his wife died."

Beatrix didn't respond as she walked toward their seats. She didn't want to miss this match. She was there to cheer on Rez. She hoped he'd relax and enjoy himself.

"Beatrix, say something." Mari rushed to keep up with her.

"Yes, it's Rez. This is his first time out in public since his wife passed."

"And he was hugging you." Jolan grinned at her. "Lucky you."

Beatrix frowned at her friend. "Jolan, lighten up. This is hard for him. He has to find his footing again."

"I'm sorry," Jolan said. "I hope it all works out for him."

Beatrix did too. She took the seat on the end. She knew she was supposed to circulate and talk to as many people as possible to clear up some of the misinformation about Indigo, but now that she was here, it was harder than she thought.

After feeling Rez's stress, her good mood had been dashed. It was important that he played well, but was that even a possibility after him being out of the game for so long?

She sat there and cheered him on. And to her relief, he appeared to her to play well. His team scored in the first chukka, otherwise known as period or quarter. The longer he played, the more he seemed to relax.

When she glanced around, she found she wasn't the only one cheering on Rez. She smiled. It was good to know that a lot of other people cared about him because he needed people to help him through this tough transition into society again.

When halftime rolled around, her friends dragged her out onto the field to stomp on divots. At first, she was worried about her new shoes, but she soon gave up worrying and instead laughed as Mari and Jolan ran around stomping on clods of dirt. It was so nice to do away with royal protocols for the moment and just have a little bit of fun. And in the end, she realized her shoes would clean up just fine.

When the match was over, Rez's team won. She wanted to congratulate him, but he never came near her again. She wondered if he was mad at her for getting him into this awkward situation. She hoped not.

He didn't want to do this.

Rez left the polo field later that afternoon. He had to keep checking his rearview mirror to make sure he wasn't being followed. At one point a motorcycle followed him for a few miles and so he made a random turn. The motorcycle tailed him through the turn and he started to worry. Was this what he was going to have to put up with every time he went into public? He hoped not.

By the second quick turn, he'd lost the motorcycle. Truth be told, he wasn't even certain it was following him. He slowed down and let his mind drift a bit.

What was up with Bea dodging his offers to meet Evi? The first time he'd offered to introduce her, he understood there hadn't been time since they'd been summoned by the Queen.

However, today when he'd suggested walking over to meet Evi, there had been a look in Bea's eyes that he wasn't able to define. Was it panic? No. Why would she be anxious about meeting his daughter? It didn't make any sense. He was missing something.

At the last minute, he made a sharp left turn. He'd been so lost in his thoughts that he'd almost missed the unmarked turnoff. Beatrix told him to come into the palace through the rear entrance, which was normally just for the staff and deliveries. They made sure to keep the press away from that entrance.

He had to stop at the gate and produce his official ID and then he was ushered onto the palace grounds. He pulled into a parking spot and then rushed inside.

He took the back steps two at a time. His daughter was supposed to be in the room next to his with the nanny on the other side of his daughter's room.

He rushed to the room and smiled when he found Evi inside. When she spotted him, she stopped playing with a teddy bear. She tossed it aside and crawled toward him. She could really move these days. It wouldn't be long until she was toddling around.

He scooped her up in his arms. "Hey, baby girl, did you have fun today?"

She said something to him but he couldn't make out her baby talk.

The nanny entered the room. The older woman with graying hair smiled when her gaze landed on Rez. "I heard her on the monitor. I didn't know you were in here."

"I just got back. Thank you for taking her to the match."

"No need to thank me. I had a lovely time."

"How are you settling in?"

Mrs. Wilson's face lit up. "It's lovely here. I had no idea the palace was so big. I mean I know we all see the photos but they don't do this place justice."

"Is there anything you need?"

She shook her head. "They have made me very comfortable here."

He nodded. "That's good." His gaze moved to his daughter. "And you seem happy." Evi uttered some baby talk. "I agree." He had no idea what he'd agreed to but his words caused Evi to smile some more and it filled his chest with warmth.

Buzz-buzz.

He thought of ignoring his phone. There was no one in particular he wanted to speak to right now. Soon enough he'd have to let Beatrix know this charade was over. He just couldn't do it. There was a reason he never tried out for plays in school—he wasn't any good at playacting.

"I can take her for you." Mrs. Wilson held out her arms to Evi, who reached out to her.

He handed over his daughter and then retrieved his phone. He looked at the caller ID. It was Istvan. At last they'd get a chance to speak.

He pressed the phone to his ear as he made his way down the hall to his suite of rooms. "Hey. How's it going?"

"Awful. I can't believe this is happening."

Rez stepped into his room and closed the door. He was confused by Istvan's answer. "You had to have a clue the press would figure out about Indigo's past, right?"

"Yes. But I was hoping it wouldn't come out until after the wedding. And then I had hoped it would blow over quickly and they'd be on to their next story."

"So where are you?"

"On Ludus Island. Indigo has friends here and she brought her mother to the private island to get away from the paparazzi."

"Is she speaking to you?" He was really worried about them. This was a lot for them to deal with just before their wedding.

"She is, but she's a bit of a nervous wreck. Not that I can blame her. Dealing with the press is a lot—especially for someone that's not used to it. She refuses to leave the island until this story blows over."

Rez raked his fingers through his hair. "What about the wedding? Is it still on?"

"I have every intention of marrying her, if she'll still have me."

Rez noticed how his friend didn't mention Indigo's feelings on the matter. Perhaps Beatrix's worry about the wedding wasn't overblown. "What can I do to help?"

"Honestly, I have no idea. If you could make this whole sordid mess go away, I'd be eternally grateful."

"I wish. Your mother has an idea about how

to deal with the paparazzi." Rez went on to tell his friend about him fake dating his sister.

"I can't believe you agreed to something that outrageous."

"You and me both. But you know I've always got your back."

"I don't know what to say." Istvan paused. "I'm sorry you've been drawn into all of this. It means so much that you're willing to help. I hope we'll be back at the palace soon."

"I'll be here."

"You're at the palace?"

"I am. Your family insisted I stay. They even invited Evi and her nanny."

"I'd like to see Evi. It's been too long since I last saw her. I bet she's grown a lot."

"She has. Hopefully you'll be back soon and then you can visit with your goddaughter."

"Thank you for everything you're doing. I know it was a lot for you to leave your home. I want you to know how much it means to me." There was a pause. "Sorry. I've got to run."

"Talk to you later."

After they ended the call, Rez was touched by his friend's words. It was then that he accepted the inevitable—he couldn't leave the palace if there was even the slightest chance the wedding would take place. He hoped their charade ended before things escalated in their fake relationship. The image of pulling Beatrix into his arms and claiming her berry-red lips with his own teased his thoughts. He couldn't help but wonder if her kiss was as sweet as he imagined.

The direction of his thoughts startled him. He couldn't believe he'd let himself imagine kissing Beatrix. She was an old friend—nothing more.

CHAPTER SIX

HOME AT LAST.

Beatrix stepped inside the palace. She'd wanted to go home right after the polo match, but her friends wouldn't hear of it. They'd wanted to hang out. And since Beatrix hadn't driven, she was along for the ride.

She wondered if Rez had returned. Then she realized there was nothing to worry about. Rez had turned into a homebody and now with his baby daughter here, he wouldn't have a reason to go out, unless it was to continue their royal charade.

She needed to talk to him about that. He had to work on acting like he was happy to see her in public. She had a feeling he'd forgotten what it was like to flirt. Back when they were kids, he had been a total flirt—though never with her. But she didn't want to get lost in thoughts of the past now.

She rushed upstairs and headed toward Rez's suite. On the way through the hallway, she noticed the door open next to Rez's room. She wondered if he was in there.

She stopped at the doorway and looked inside. She didn't see Rez. But then her gaze landed on the white crib between the two tall windows. It was so strange to see a crib in the palace. In fact, she'd never seen a crib in the palace. She had been too young when Cecelia was born to recall it.

All of the sudden there was movement within the crib. Beatrix told herself she should just move along, but there was this curiosity to see his baby. She took a step into the room. She couldn't help but wonder if Evi favored her father, with his dark good looks.

She hesitated just inside the doorway. She didn't want to disturb the baby. After all, she knew absolutely nothing about babies. Her friends were only starting to get married. No one was having babies yet. And now that Beatrix knew she couldn't have children, she avoided babies at all costs because they reminded her of what she couldn't have. It was also part of the reason she'd decided to take a year off from dating.

She didn't want to draw someone else into her fertility issues. If things got serious, it would be asking too much of a person to deal with her diagnosis. The risk of the relationship falling apart was too great and made her all the more determined to cling to her single status.

However, she hadn't missed the way Rez lighted up when he was with his daughter. Evi was the only person who could make him truly smile. He was such a fabulous father. Rez deserved to have more children with the right woman when he was ready to move on.

She could imagine Rez with a little one pulling at his leg while he held a baby in his arms. The image pulled at the scars on her heart. An image like that would never include her.

Evi's head popped up over the side of the crib. She stood there with her dark curls and blue eyes, staring at her. Evi was absolutely adorable.

Wait. Was Evi smiling at her? She was. Warmth swelled within Beatrix's chest and radiated outward. Soon the baby's smile turned into a drooling fest, all over the crib rail.

Beatrix glanced around for the nanny. She didn't see her anywhere. In fact, there didn't seem to be anyone around.

"Goo-goo." Evi held on to the rail and then jumped. She fell back.

Beatrix's breath hitched in her throat. She instinctively rushed forward. *Please let her be okay.* She peered in the crib. Evi looked up at her and laughed.

"Thank goodness. You had me worried." As Evi stared up at her with her rosy lips lifted in a smile that plumped up her cheeks, pain arrowed into Beatrix's heart.

She would never have this experience with her own child. For so long, she'd convinced herself that she didn't want children—that she had a full life. But now she realized it wasn't the truth. Tears pricked the back of her eyes. She blinked them away.

Evi rolled over. She crawled over and once more used the rails to help her stand.

"You don't want to do that," Beatrix said. "You're going to fall again." She watched as the little girl began to jump again. "Be careful. No more jumping, okay?"

Beatrix glanced around, hoping someone would come help out. Where was Rez? She looked at Evi, who was smiling as she stood there.

"Evi, no more jumping. Okay?"

As though Evi understood only the word *jump*, the little girl began bouncing again. Beatrix's body tensed with worry. Not wanting Evi to hurt herself, Beatrix automatically reached out. Just as she was about to pick up Evi, she hesitated.

"Evi…" Rez walked into the room. He came to a stop when he saw Beatrix standing there. "Bea, I didn't expect to find you here."

"I…uh…was looking for you." Beatrix backed away from the crib. "And then Evi's door was open."

"I was in the kitchen getting her a bottle." He held up a full bottle of milk. "Thank you for checking in on her."

"Um… Yes. No problem."

"She loves to jump. She's going to have the strongest legs."

Beatrix's gaze narrowed. "How did you know she was jumping?"

He held up his other hand, which was holding a baby monitor.

"Oh." Heat warmed her cheeks. "So you heard us?"

He nodded. "I'm glad you two finally met. Please feel free to visit her anytime. She loves to be around people."

"I didn't mean to intrude on her dinner."

He set the bottle down. "You didn't. And I mean it, you're welcome to visit her whenever you want."

"Thanks."

Evi cooed. She jumped up and down, obviously excited to see her father.

"Anyway," Beatrix said. "I…I'll just be going."

She started for the door. When she passed him, he reached out and gently touched her arm. "You don't have to leave."

"I should. You, um…need time with your daughter." This situation was just too cozy. The baby was so cute. And Rez was much too handsome. Sometimes it was tough to remember that he was a grieving widower.

Her legs moved quickly as she slipped out the door. It wasn't until she made it along the hallway and down the staircase that she took her first easy breath.

"Are you okay?"

Beatrix jumped. Pressing a hand to her chest, she turned to find Gisella standing there, giving her a puzzled look. "I'm fine."

Her sister arched a brow. "Are you sure?"

"Yes." Not really but she wasn't going to get into any of that with her older sister. "Why?"

"The way you rushed down the steps, it was like you were running from something or someone."

"Don't be silly." She attempted to sound calm and relaxed. Wanting to change the subject to anything but herself, she asked, "What are you doing here? I would have thought they'd have you holed away in a meeting."

Gisella sighed. "I escaped. There's only so much I can absorb at one time." She moved closer to Beatrix. "Can I be honest with you?"

Beatrix had no idea what Gisella was about to confess, but she had to admit she was curious. Her older sister wasn't one for confiding in people so Beatrix had no idea what to expect from her.

"Of course you can. What is it?"

"I never knew there was so much to learn to become the Sovereign. It's so much more than I ever expected." Gisella sighed again. "I better get back to it."

And with that Gisella turned on her heels and set off toward the back of the palace, leaving Beatrix alone with her thoughts. They immediately returned to Rez and Evi. She wasn't so sure what had happened back in the nursery or why it had unnerved her so much. She just knew she needed to keep her distance.

He wasn't alone.

Rez had never seen Bea so spooked. It was like she couldn't get out of the nursery fast enough. He had no idea what had freaked her out.

He suspected it was the same thing that had gotten to him—this fake relationship. It was just too much for the both of them. He never should have agreed to it.

There had to be another way to stem off the stories about Istvan and Indigo. He'd been giving it some thought and he had some ideas. He wanted to run them by Beatrix, but when he'd stopped by her room, she hadn't been there.

It didn't help that the palace was so large a person could hide and not be found for the longest time. He had a feeling as Evi got a bit older she'd be thrilled to play hide-and-seek within the palace walls.

He'd returned to the nursery to find his baby girl standing in her crib, waiting for him to pick her up. "Aren't you sleepy yet?"

Evi jumped as though she knew exactly what he'd said.

"Sir, would you like me to take her for you?" Mrs. Wilson asked.

He was torn between staying for his favorite part of Evi's day—rocking her to sleep— or continuing to track down Bea. He'd never experienced this sort of dilemma before. Back at his estate, he didn't have distractions. He'd had all the time in the world for Evi.

He glanced up. "You don't mind?"

A smile lit up the nanny's face. "I never mind rocking such a sweet baby to sleep. Besides, I don't have much else to do here."

Perhaps this was the answer to his problem. He picked up Evi, who started to fuss because she was tired. He held her in front of him, so she could see him. "I love you, baby girl. Sleep tight." He gave his daughter a kiss on her chubby cheeks and then handed her over. "If you have any problems getting her down, message me and I'll come back."

"We'll be fine. Don't you worry."

"Thank you for everything. I really appreciate you making the trip."

"I'm honored to be here."

Rez leaned over to his daughter again. "You be good." He took one of her little hands in his own and kissed it. "And have sweet dreams."

He walked to the doorway, where he paused and glanced back. Mrs. Wilson had moved to the crib, undoubtedly in order to change Evi into a fresh diaper and her pajamas. Knowing he wouldn't be far away, he moved on.

He made his way back to Bea's suite of rooms. He knocked but once again there was no answer.

He reached for his phone and messaged her.

Where are you? We need to talk.

Seconds ticked by as he waited for a response. The seconds turned to minutes while he paced in the hallway. Just when he thought she wasn't going to get back to him, his phone dinged.

Do you want to meet in the library?

Yes. Heading there now.

He moved in that direction. It was on the main floor and down a hallway. Lucky for him, he'd spent a lot of time in the palace when he was growing up. Otherwise it would be so easy to get lost in a place as big as this one.

When he stepped into the library, he expected to find Bea waiting for him. It appeared he was the one waiting for her—again. While he waited for her to arrive, he practiced what he'd say to her. He'd give her a reasonable alternative to them trying to fool the paparazzi, one that didn't include him. And then he would scoop up his daughter and head home until he was needed here for the wedding. He couldn't wait to get on the road.

A couple of minutes later Bea walked in. She closed the double doors behind her. "What did you need to see me about?"

This was his chance to sell her on his plan. "We need to do something different."

"I agree."

"You do?" He was confused. He thought she was all invested in them creating a fake romance.

"Yes. I think we need to push up our time-line. Instead of waiting until Friday, we need to see each other in public tomorrow."

He shook his head. "I don't think that's the change we need."

She pressed a hand to her hip—her gently rounded hip. He swallowed hard. When had Bea gotten all of these curves? She'd definitely grown and filled out in all of the right places.

"What do you have in mind?"

"I think we need to give up this charade. I don't think anyone is interested in us."

"What makes you say that?"

"Because I didn't receive any notifications on my phone from anyone. I don't think the public cares."

"And I think we're just getting started. It was only the first day. You have to give it time. It was supposed to be subtle. It's not like you can just walk up to me and kiss me. What would be the story in that?"

He swallowed hard again. *Kiss her?* This wasn't going to happen. No way. "Since when am I supposed to kiss you?"

She frowned at him. "You don't have to sound like it is the worst thing in the world."

"That's not what I meant. It's just that it's you and me. We're not like that." They'd never been romantically linked.

Years ago, Bea had been too young for him. And then he met Enora. The timing had never been right. But now things were different. And then there was the idea that Bea could be a mother to his little girl.

The breath hitched in his throat. Had that thought really crossed his mind? It struck him with its enormity. Was he prepared to go that far to give Evi a family? He didn't have an answer to that question.

"What are we like?" Bea's voice drew him back to their conversation.

He averted his gaze. "You know."

"No, I don't know. Please tell me."

Was that a frown on her face? Why was she getting upset with him? She couldn't be any more comfortable with this arrangement than him.

He shifted his weight from one foot to the other as he tried to guess at how she envisioned their relationship. "Well, you know, you're like my little sister. Just like when we were kids."

"Kids? If you haven't noticed I've grown up, just like you."

He raked his fingers through his hair. He

could see quite clearly that she was very much a woman with all of the curvy goodness that went along with it.

The problem was he didn't want to see her that way. He shouldn't see her that way. He was a widower—a single father. Romance was not on his radar. He didn't know if it would ever be something he would want again. And if he was to propose they create a family for Evi, would Bea insist on romance?

Of course, there was Istvan to consider. He would be very upset about Rez having any sort of relationship with Bea. Istvan had told him in no uncertain terms that his sisters— all three of them—were off-limits to Rez. Of course, back before Enora had entered his life, he had been known as a playboy. The love-'em-and-leave-'em type. Enora had changed all of that.

Now Bea wanted him to act like he had a lifetime ago. He didn't want to go back. He wasn't even sure he knew how to go back and be that carefree guy.

Today hadn't gone well.

Beatrix would be the first person to admit it, but that didn't mean they should give up. They were not giving up. This was much too important for them to stop now. They had to push forward.

The information from her brother was that Indigo was refusing to come back to the palace—to deal with the hurtful headlines. It was a lot for someone to take on, especially if they weren't used to having their lives dissected in the news.

It was a lot for Beatrix and she'd grown up in the spotlight. But she also knew how to use the press to her advantage. And that's exactly what they were going to do now. She just had to get Rez back on board.

"We can't stop now," she said. "Trust me. By spoon-feeding the paparazzi, it'll only make them more curious about us."

Rez didn't say anything. He looked as though he was staring off into space. He was probably thinking of some way to get out of this awkward situation.

"Rez?" When he didn't respond, she spoke louder. "Rez, did you hear me?"

"Uh… Yeah."

Ding.

He checked his phone. "It's yours."

Beatrix knew it was her phone. She'd felt it vibrate in her pocket, but she didn't want an interruption now. When Rez sent her an expectant look as her phone sounded again, she reluctantly reached for it.

It was an alert from the *Duchess Tales*. They'd just posted something. She read the title: Back in the Saddle Again...

"Bea, is something wrong?" Concern rang out in Rez's voice.

"*Duchess Tales* posted something." She pressed on the link in order to read more.

The popular site was known to post at all hours of the day or night with "breaking" news. They had sources everywhere and it was amazing the amount of information they were able to gather and at such great speed. Sometimes there was news about the royal family posted even before all of the members of the family had been notified about the matter.

"What did they say?" Interest rang out in his voice.

She read him the headline.

"I take it this article is about me?" He didn't sound impressed.

"I don't know. Let me read it."

This most devoted royal watcher has the most exciting news for all of you single ladies out there...and maybe some of you who aren't so single! *eye-wink emoji*

Ladies, ladies, be still your galloping hearts, but this royal watcher can now verify that the sexy Duke of Kaspar has gotten back on his polo pony.

There was a photo of Rez on his horse. Beatrix stared at it for a moment, unable to turn away from the image. It took her a moment to realize what was so different about him in the photo. And then she realized it was the first time since he'd returned to the palace that he looked relaxed. Even the stress lines on his face were soothed.

With concerted effort, she continued to read the post. All the while she hoped the ruse was beginning to work.

This royal follower also has a new update on the fake princess front. It appears the wannabe princess's father stole from the palace. No one knows whether it was royal jewels or just some other priceless relic, but he and his family were found out and banished from all of Rydiania. Apparently the shame was too much for him to bear because he ended his life shortly after, leaving his family to deal with the shame. Oh, my. We do reap what we sow, don't we?

Beatrix's stomach plummeted. How did they come up with these blatant lies? Did they not know what damage they do to people? For once, she was relieved that Indigo and Istvan weren't here. Hopefully they weren't checking the press either.

She was afraid to keep reading. She had no idea what other painful lies were going to be flung about and quoted as the truth. Ha! There was barely any truth to be found here and yet many of Rydania's residents read this blogsite religiously.

And if Prince Istvan calls off his marriage to the wannabe, he'll be back on the market too. Oh, ladies, this summer is turning out to be most amazing. Dust off your slinkiest dresses and most glamorous heels, it's time to go bachelor hunting.

Beatrix huffed. Who was this royal watcher? And why were they out to ruin Istvan's happiness? If she knew who was behind the *Duchess Tales*, she would go to them and demand they write retractions. The wedding was going to happen. It had to happen because they truly loved each other. And it wasn't right for the court of public opinion to ruin it.

Though Beatrix was known to hold her

tongue while with her family, when someone came after her loved ones, she would defend them with vigor. But without a name, she was left helpless and reading these outrageous stories.

Who shall win the hearts of our two most eligible bachelors? Well, I can't tell you that. In the Duke's case, it certainly won't be Princess Beatrix.

There was a photo of her with Rez. He was frowning at her and she was frowning back. Oh, no! This wasn't good. Not good at all.

That is it for now, royal followers. Know that I am hard at work digging up the truth about Prince Istvan's status. I know you ladies want your chance to win his heart and you just might get your chance.

As for the Duke, we'll be on the lookout for him too. Now that he's out of mourning and back in the social arena, I have a feeling his social calendar is going to runneth over with invites.

Keep in touch, my lovely royal followers. I will share the details as they unfold. Until next time...xox

Beatrix turned to Rez but he apparently got tired of waiting for her to tell him what was in the post and instead he'd pulled it up on his phone.

Just then Gisella came rushing into the library. "Did you see what the Duchess wrote?"

"I just read it." Beatrix gestured to Rez with her head. "He's reading it now."

"It's getting worse." Gisella huffed. "We have to do more."

"That's just what I was telling Rez. It's too late tonight for a social function, but I know tomorrow there's a showing at the gallery in the village. They draw in a lot of big names now that the word is out that our brother is a big buyer there."

"Good idea. But how are you going to get more press coverage? They basically wrote off anything romantic between you and Rez."

"Agreed." Rez's voice held an agitated tone. "How are you going to change the narrative?"

Beatrix's mind searched for the answer to that question and came up empty. She kept coming back to her original plan, only with an escalated timeline.

She turned to her sister. "You need to speed up the palace's formal release about Indigo and her family."

"But it's royal protocol not to rush to respond to the lies in the press."

"Who cares about protocol? By the time the palace gets around to putting out a royal statement, our brother's wedding will be officially called off. Is that what you want?"

Gisella shook her head. "But they aren't going to like making an exception to the protocol."

"And they like the hurtful lies being spewed about by the Duchess?"

"You do have a point," Gisella said.

"Good. Talk to the King, have him put some people on the statement tonight. Once the public has the truth, hopefully the story will die away."

"And what about you two?" Gisella arched a brow as her gaze moved between Beatrix and Rez. "There's no way anyone is going to believe the chance of a possible romance with photos of you two frowning at each other."

"Agreed." Beatrix couldn't argue. They had to do better. "We'll work on that while you work on the formal statement."

Gisella nodded. "Getting the palace to break protocol isn't going to be as easy as you seem to think it will be."

She nodded in agreement. "Neither will faking a relationship. Now go."

Gisella huffed. "I'm going. Since when did I become the errand girl?"

"Don't think of it as an errand. Think of it as helping your brother, who is in dire need of assistance."

Gisella turned and left.

Beatrix turned to Rez. He stood there studying her with a strange look on his handsome face. "What? Is there something on my face?"

He shook his head. "I just never saw this side of you."

"What side?"

"The pushy, in-charge, don't-mess-with-me side." He sent her a smile. "Bea, you've really have grown up."

The name grated on her nerves and it didn't help when his deep chuckle followed. Her lips pressed together as her back teeth ground together. No one laughed at her, not since she was a little kid.

"This isn't a time for your amusement. We have a big problem, if you hadn't noticed."

The amusement was erased from his voice. "I've noticed. And I think we're making a big mistake if we do the same thing we did yesterday."

"I agree." When the surprise shone in his eyes, she continued. "That's why tomorrow you actually have to look happy to see me. No frowns allowed."

"I didn't frown," he grumbled.

"Do I need to pull up the photo?"

"No, no. But you were frowning too."

"Because you were frustrating me." He had a habit of doing it, like now. "So tomorrow we have a date to meet up at the Durand Gallery."

"I still think this is a mistake."

What she heard him say was that he didn't want to pretend to be in a relationship with her. He couldn't be any more obvious. She told herself that it was because he was grieving his wife. She shouldn't take it personally, but it still hurt.

CHAPTER SEVEN

THIS WAS A waste of time.

Nothing they did was going to fix the horrid headlines.

And still Rez dressed nicely. He proceeded to drive into the village. What he hadn't expected when he arrived was the village to be so busy that he couldn't find a parking spot near the gallery. It appeared Bea hadn't been exaggerating when she said the gallery was popular.

At least the evening wouldn't be a total waste. He might even find a piece of art for his home. He wanted to surround Evi with beautiful artwork. He liked to think that's what her mother would have done but he didn't truly know.

The plan was for him to leave the palace first and allow Bea to make a grand entrance. He didn't know what she was planning but it wouldn't matter. She could wear a trash bag and she would still turn heads.

At the door stood a tall, muscular bodyguard wearing a black suit with a black shirt and tie. In his hand, he held a digital notebook. He stood between Rez and the door. Without lifting his head, the man asked, "Name?"

"The Duke of Kaspar."

Immediately the man's head lifted. His dark eyes widened. "I'm sorry, sir. I didn't realize it was you." He pulled open the door. "Please go in."

"Have a good evening." Rez stepped into the gallery.

He had never been in here before. The gallery had a clean look with white walls and a slate-gray floor. While dozens of well-dressed people milled about with drinks in their hands, he skirted around the edge of the showroom. He did his best to ignore how people's heads turned as he passed by.

His gaze moved to the walls, which were covered with colorful canvases. It wouldn't be hard to find something here to purchase. The problem might be narrowing it down to one...or two pieces of art.

He stepped around one of the illuminated vitrines that held small hand-carved figurines. The vitrines were strategically placed throughout the large room with various works of art from jewelry to sculptures.

He walked over to a wall in order to have

a closer look at an oil painting. It was a field of purple wildflowers. When he studied it, he could easily imagine being in the field with a soft breeze that carried with it the perfume of the flowers as the sunshine warmed his face. This was the type of art he wanted to stimulate Evi's imagination. He made a mental note of the painting so he could purchase it.

"Hey, Rez. It's so good to see you."

He turned around to find a woman with shoulder-length auburn hair smiling at him. He knew he should know her name, but he couldn't recall it. If Bea was here, she could discreetly let him know the woman's name.

"Hello." He tried to think of an excuse to move on.

The next thing he knew, the woman was wrapping her arms around him. Her strong, sweet perfume wrapped around him, smothering him. Her cherry red lips pressed to his cheek.

It took him a second to detach himself. Her arms were more like octopus tentacles that didn't want to let him go. His gaze desperately searched the room for Bea. Figures, she chose tonight to be late.

"I'm so sorry about your wife." The woman spoke in a high-pitched tone. "It must be so hard raising a baby on your own."

He inwardly groaned. This was the very last conversation he wanted to have with a stranger. Not knowing what to say, he nodded his head.

"What you need is a new wife—someone to help you out with your daughter and that big house of yours." Her smile brightened.

Surely this woman, who was obviously at least ten years older than him, wasn't suggesting he was just going to up and marry her. He couldn't think of anything he wanted to do less.

"If you'll excuse me, I see someone I need to have a word with." He had no one in particular that he wanted to speak to but at this point, he would walk out and have an hour-long conversation with the bodyguard at the front door before he would stand here with this woman a minute longer.

"Rez!" Someone caught his arm.

He stopped and turned. It was a blonde. He knew her from years ago. Her name was… "Hello, Liz."

A big smile lifted her cheeks. "I didn't know you would be here tonight."

"It was a last-minute decision." And one he hadn't personally made. Bea had insisted their appearance here would be noticed.

Speaking of the Princess, his gaze moved

around the room. Where was she? Sure, they didn't want to show up at the same time, but it would be nice if they'd show up within the same hour.

Liz linked her arm with his like she had some claim on him. The move made him extremely uncomfortable. He wasn't ready to get cozy with anyone—especially someone he barely knew.

Right now, he was struggling with his new life. He needed to stay focused on doing his best for his daughter. And it would really help if Bea was here to make this evening a little easier.

"It's so good that you're here. We've really missed you. It was such a shame about your wife. I can't even imagine what it must be like with her here one minute and gone the next. Your poor little girl."

He wanted to tell the woman to shut up. His wife was not a subject to be bantered around at a social engagement. And it wasn't a subject he wanted to discuss with anyone—especially her.

Where are you, Bea?

As though his desperation had summoned her, Bea glided into the gallery. *Wow!* That's all he could think.

Bea was a knockout. He wasn't the only

one to notice. A hush fell over the crowd as heads turned in her direction. As though Bea was used to being in the spotlight, she paused. Her photo was taken and then she was greeted by person after person.

Her long dark hair was down with the loose curls flowing over her shoulder. His fingers tingled with the desire to comb his fingers through those long locks. Her makeup was soft, just enough to highlight her natural beauty. Her lips were painted with a wine-colored gloss that drew his attention and held it a moment longer than necessary.

She wore a white lace blouse with loose flowy sleeves. The gaps in the material of the sleeves gave a teasing glimpse of her creamy white skin.

He should turn away but he couldn't move. His feet were planted to the ground. A white skirt fit snuggly against her curvy hips and ended a few centimeters above her knees.

Her blue heels made her toned legs look as though they went on forever. Rez swallowed hard. The Bea he used to know never looked this hot. He would have remembered that.

"Excuse me." He didn't wait for Liz to respond as he made his way toward Bea.

By the time he reached her side, she was surrounded by three other men. One was much too young for her. Another was much too old. And that left one other man to send him a challenging look. Rez wasn't the least bit intimidated. Even if he didn't have prior plans to meet up with Bea here, he still wouldn't have worried about gaining her attention.

After all, they were very old friends. Their friendship went back so far that he recalled her learning to ride her first bike. She'd insisted he hold on to the back of the bike so she wouldn't fall over. That memory felt like a million years ago.

Bea laughed at something the kid said to her. And all Rez could think who that he wanted her to laugh at something he said—he wanted to make her smile and put the sparkle in her eyes. As soon as the thought came to him, he stopped it.

What was he doing? He was in no position to want a woman to smile for him—to find her exceedingly attractive. He'd already had one beautiful, sweet wife and he'd let her down. He didn't deserve another chance at happiness.

Not wanting to get caught up in the painful memories, he focused on his task. He moved to Bea's side and said loud enough for the other men to overhear, "Your Highness, may I have a moment of your time?"

Bea turned her head and bestowed a warm smile on him. "The Duke of Kaspar. It's so good to see you again. Of course you can."

She said it so convincingly that for a moment he thought she was truly happy to see him. And it made his pulse pick up its pace. It took him a moment to remember that everything said between them was for show—nothing more. And that's how it should be because there was absolutely zero chance of anything real ever happening between them. He wouldn't let it happen.

He was frowning…again.

Beatrix struggled not to sigh in exasperation. What was it with Rez? Every time he saw her, he would frown. Was she that displeasing to look at?

She was late this evening because she'd taken extra care in picking out the perfect outfit to wear. She wanted something that wasn't too businesslike or too casual.

She'd really hoped she'd got the right combination, but the frown on Rez's face was having her rethink her choices—even if it was too late to do anything about it now.

Instead she turned her attention to the gallery. She'd visited it many times in the past.

She loved the tranquility within these walls—today she didn't feel so tranquil.

She let Rez set the pace as they made their way through the gallery. There were many heads turning their way. Most of them were women and they were frowning. Perhaps their ruse was starting to take root. She couldn't wait to read *Duchess Tales* later that evening.

She leaned in close to Rez. "The palace's statement was released this afternoon. That's part of the reason I was late. I was reading the press coverage. So far there's no response from the Duchess."

"I haven't heard anyone mention Istvan or Indigo since I've been here so maybe the release is working and we can forget about our endeavor."

She slipped her hand in the crook of his arm. "You're much too eager to give up on our ruse. I'm beginning to think you don't like me."

He glanced her way. "You aren't serious, are you?"

She shrugged. "You certainly frown enough when I'm around."

"I do not." He frowned at her.

"Really? Because you're doing it right now."

He sighed. "Shall we look at some of the work?"

"Certainly. I love to see all of the new pieces."

And so they walked together, looking at the artwork. She left her hand in the crook of his arm, warning off some of the eager young ladies that for the moment Rez was taken. And it worked. They were given a modicum of privacy as they discussed the various pieces of art.

She was delighted to find Rez was earnestly searching for artwork for his home. This was something she could help him with. "If you like the wildflower painting, you should check out some of Indigo's work. It's just around this corner."

They made their way past a large group of people and turned the corner. Beatrix came to a sudden stop.

Rez bumped into her. "Sorry."

She stared at the empty wall. Where were Indigo's paintings? Had they all sold? Part of her was excited for her future sister-in-law. Another part of her was disappointed that she couldn't share Indi's amazing work with Rez.

Just then an older woman with short dark hair and a pleasant smile approached them. She quickly bowed to Beatrix. "Your Highness, it's so good to have you here."

"Esme, it's so good to see you." She smiled at the sweet woman. "I'd like to introduce you to the Duke of Kaspar. Rez, this is Esme Durand. She and her husband own the gallery."

"It's a pleasure to meet you," Esme said.

"Your gallery is wonderful. I intend to purchase a couple of pieces. I'm having a hard time figuring out which paintings are my favorite."

"It can be quite the challenge." Esme beamed.

"I was just about to show the Duke some of Indigo's work, but the wall where her work normally hangs is empty," Beatrix said. "Did it all sell?"

The smile fell from Esme's face. Her brows drew together as she glanced away and pursed her lips.

Beatrix grew concerned. "Esme, what is it?"

She lifted her gaze to meet Beatrix's. "We had a problem earlier this week with someone trying to vandalize the paintings. We decided to move them to the back until things settle down."

Beatrix gasped. "That's horrible."

Esme nodded. "We had to call the authorities. Some people are just so awful. I saw the release from the palace this afternoon. It should put a stop to the awful lies that have been running rampant."

"We hope so. And thank you for protecting Indigo's work. Since Rez is looking for a piece of art, I wanted to show him Indigo's work. I think she has a piece that might be just right for him."

"Certainly." Esme explained exactly where they could find the pieces.

With the aid of Esme's directions, they found the artwork in an employee's-only area of the gallery. It was such a shame the pieces had to be put back here for safekeeping. Now everyone at the show would miss out on seeing these fine works.

"That's really nice." Rez gestured to a painting of an older woman surrounded by kittens as she tried to feed them.

"I'm afraid that one is sold," Beatrix said.

"How can you tell which ones are sold?" Rez asked.

She moved to a painting beside it. "See the red tag?" When he nodded, she said, "It means the piece is still available for sale. They remove the tag after it's been sold."

He continued moving along the wall, taking in the various painting of people from all walks of life and all ages. When he came to a beach scene, he stopped and stared. This was the piece Beatrix was certain he would like. The painting had a little girl with a bonnet on playing in the sand.

He turned to her. "That could be a painting of Evi at the beach."

She smiled and nodded. "I had a feeling you would say that."

"And it has a red tag." Rez looked quite pleased. "I haven't taken Evi to the beach yet."

"You should do it. She'll love it."

His brow furrowed. "You don't think she's too young?"

Beatrix hesitated. "I think you'd be the best judge of that."

There was so much she didn't know about babies, but there was a part of her that would love to learn. She tamped down that desire. It wouldn't do her well to dwell on things that weren't going to happen.

As they returned to the front of the gallery, Rez let Esme know which paintings he wanted to purchase. Afterward, they made their way slowly around the gallery, taking in all the many pieces of art.

The evening flew by much too quickly. She'd thoroughly enjoyed Rez's company. It was as though something had changed and tonight he was fun and engaging. He was very much like the Rez she used to know.

And then the time came when she needed to go about doing her royal responsibility. "I don't want to, but I should go mingle."

It was her duty to start answering questions about the palace's statement. The sooner they had the correct information out there, the sooner the outlandish rumors would die down.

Rez nodded. "I understand. I enjoyed viewing the gallery with you."

She smiled. "I enjoyed it too."

She didn't say it to him, but this evening hadn't felt like work. Instead it was pleasant to spend time with him. It almost felt like a real date. She reminded herself that he was only putting on a show for the public. The thought dampened her mood.

Beatrix turned and walked away. She was anxious to get home and read the *Duchess Tales* write-up. Thanks to Rez, their evening had gone so much better than the polo match. It had almost fooled her.

CHAPTER EIGHT

HAD IT WORKED?

Had they succeeded in snaring the paparazzi's attention?

Beatrix had been anxious to leave the gallery after spotting Rez walking out the front door with a wrapped package under his arm. She so wanted to leave with him, but she knew she couldn't.

First, she had misinformation to dispel. Second, she didn't want to rush their relationship—in the press, of course. It wasn't like they had a real relationship aside from being old friends.

But she had noticed how the women nearly salivated when he was in their proximity. Of course, she couldn't blame them. He was so handsome—even more so than when they were kids. The years had given him a level of maturity that she found downright sexy.

And so Beatrix stayed at the gallery, making her rounds. There were questions and more questions about Istvan and Indigo. She was floored at some of the more straightforward questions, like was the palace lying to cover up Indigo's arrest record? *What arrest record?* Indigo was never on the wrong side of the law.

Beatrix talked and talked, hoping the information she shared here would be spread among the attendees' friends. It was amazing how the press could take something and twist it until it didn't even represent the truth.

Thankfully, after clarifying matters, most people believed her. And they felt sorry for Indigo and Istvan. Beatrix wondered if perhaps the palace should do a public address to further clarify matters. The King could give a Kingdom-wide address. It'd be like he was coming into people's homes and having a personal chat with them, much like Beatrix had done this evening.

With most people having departed, Beatrix thanked the hosts and made her way back to the palace. On her short ride to the palace, she checked the *Duchess Tales* website. There were still no new posts that day. What were they waiting for?

With a huff, Beatrix stuffed her phone back in her purse. Her feet ached and she was tempted to kick off her new heels. But she knew if she were to do that she would never get the shoes back on. She would have to wait a while longer to go barefoot.

First, she wanted to meet up with Rez and compare notes about the evening. As her driver maneuvered the car up the long drive to the palace, Beatrix pulled out her phone. Her fingers moved rapidly over the screen as she messaged Rez.

Can we meet in the library?

I can't.

We really need to talk.

Come to the nursery.

The nursery? It wasn't exactly the place she wanted to have a serious conversation. But it seemed as though Rez wasn't giving her many options. Still, that didn't stop her from trying again.

We need to talk privately.

Agreed. Let's meet in the nursery.

Fine. Let me change and I'll see you.

We'll be waiting.

She could imagine him with Evi in his arms. When he was with her, it was like his troubles faded away. Instead of frowning, he was always smiling. The baby was good for him. Beatrix just couldn't help but wish he shared some of those smiles with her.

After the car dropped her off, she entered the palace through the back door. As soon as she was inside, she slipped off her heels. She sighed in relief. With them dangling from her fingertips, she rushed up the back stairs.

She changed into a comfortable pair of blue shorts and a white lacy top. She checked her phone again. She was starting to think there wasn't going to be an update from the Duchess that day. She wondered what that meant. She didn't know if it was a good sign or not.

She moved to the guest wing where Rez's set of rooms were located. Once more the nursery door was open. Since she was still in her bare feet, her steps were muffled.

When she reached the doorway, she paused. Rez held Evi in his arms. His back was to Beatrix. He was singing a lullaby. Beatrix knew she should make her presence known but she couldn't bring herself to ruin this moment.

Who knew that Rez had such a beautifully deep voice? She certainly didn't. In all of the years she'd known him, she'd never heard him sing. And the baby seemed totally entranced with her father's voice.

He danced around. When he spun around, he spotted Beatrix. She expected him to stop singing as soon as he saw her but instead his gaze connected with hers as he continued to softly sing.

In that moment, her heart swooned. There was nothing sweeter than Rez with a baby in his arms. He looked so natural. And the baby was all smiles.

It also reminded her of what she was never going to have. Tears stung the backs of her eyes. She blinked repeatedly. She couldn't stay here and let him see her tears. She turned on her heels and set off down the hallway.

"Bea, wait!" Rez called after her.

She kept going. She swiped at the dampness on her cheeks. Why would he invite her to speak with him in the nursery if all he was planning to do was sing songs? Didn't he understand that they had important things to discuss?

What in the world?

He might have been married and had a daughter, but Rez still didn't understand women. Not really. He thought things were going all right between him and Bea.

He'd even thought they had a good evening. It hadn't started that way for him, but after Bea showed up, he started to relax and to enjoy his time at the gallery. He'd thought she'd enjoyed it too.

But now as Rez stood in the hallway, he watched Bea's stiff shoulders and her ramrod-straight back as she strode away. And he didn't understand what had happened.

Granted his singing wasn't that good, but Evi hadn't complained. Something else must have upset Bea, but he had no idea what was bothering her. Maybe there had been something posted online about them or her brother.

"Bea, wait." He tried once more. "Please."

She didn't so much as give him a backward glance. She turned a corner and disappeared from sight.

"Sir, I heard you. Is everything all right?" Mrs. Wilson approached him with a worried look on her face.

"I, ah, need to speak with the Princess. Would you be able to take Evi?"

"Certainly." The nanny held out her arms for the baby.

"Thank you."

As soon as his daughter was secure in the

nanny's arms, Rez took off after Bea. He had to know what had happened to make her take off like that. He was so confused.

The only problem was that he had no idea where she'd gone. Was she upstairs? Downstairs? He opted to check her suite of rooms.

When he reached her door, he rapped his knuckles on the door. She didn't immediately answer. Still, he waited. He needed to fix the problem. She was his only true ally in the palace with Istvan being away.

He knocked again. "Bea, it's me. Open up."

The door swung open and she frowned at him. "What do you want?"

The hostile tone of her voice had him taking a step back. What was wrong with her? Had something happened when she'd left the art gallery alone?

"To check on you. Why did you leave the nursery?" He wanted to ask why she seemed to be mad at him, but he couldn't let himself do it. He couldn't let her know that her feelings toward him mattered.

"You were busy." Her gaze didn't quite meet his.

"You could have joined us. From what I remember, you have a decent voice." She had a beautiful voice, but he wasn't going there either.

She shook her head. "I didn't want to intrude on a family moment."

"Well, there's no family moment now. Should we talk?"

She hesitated, which was not common for her. Something was definitely off with her, but he still didn't have a clue what it was or what it was about.

"Maybe we should talk in the morning."

He didn't understand this sudden change in her attitude. Up until now she was pushing for them to work on their plans—to perfect their ruse with the paparazzi. Now something had suddenly changed.

And then he had the worst thought. "Did Istvan and Indigo call off their wedding?"

"What? No. Why would you think that?"

He sighed as he shifted his weight from one foot to the other and then back again. "Then I don't understand."

"Understand what?"

Really? She was going to play it that way? Then he was going to have to be the one that was direct. "I don't understand why you were the one that pushed me into this ruse and now you are the one backing out of it."

"I am not." Her words were firm and swift.

"Then shouldn't we talk?"

Ding.

Bea moved away from the doorway while leaving the door cracked open. She picked up her phone. "It's a new post from *Duchess Tales*."

He stepped into the room. "What does it say?"

"Let me pull it up." She started to read to herself.

"Out loud."

Without lifting her gaze from the phone, she said, "The headline reads, A Wedding in Shambles."

This wasn't good. Not good at all. And he wasn't one to worry, but even he had to admit that things were getting worse.

Bea's voice drew his attention as she continued to read.

According to my source, who has access to the palace, Prince Istvan and Indigo are no longer in residence. They have fled Rydiania for parts unknown.

If that doesn't say the wedding is off, I don't know what does. If the palace wasn't covering something up, why run?

Bea stopped reading and looked at him. "How do they know all of this?"

"Is it possible they have a spy within the

palace walls?" He didn't like the thought. It was hard enough living a life in the public eye without having to worry about being watched at home—even if your home was a palace.

"I don't know. I never thought of it. I do know that everyone who is hired must sign an ironclad nondisclosure agreement. But I'm not aware of any new hires."

"We can figure that out later. What else does it say?"

While we await the reappearance of the Prince...and perhaps Indigo...we have other royal news. The Duke of Kaspar was once again out and about. This time he was spotted at the Durand Art Gallery...

Rez's body tensed. He hated having the spotlight on him and his life. And if he didn't owe his oldest friend a *huge* debt, he wouldn't take part in this ruse.

It seems as though now that he's reentered society that he isn't going to let any dust settle on his shoes. This evening he was spotted talking to numerous women. Funnily enough, he was so busy with the female guests that he didn't have time to speak with any of the

males. Was this intentional, ladies? Or is he
on the hunt for a new duchess?

Bea stopped reading and glanced up at him.
"I'm sorry."

He brushed off her apology, even though
the words poked at the scar upon his heart.
"It's not your fault what that horrible woman
writes."

"I don't have to read any more."

"Of course you do." He could get through
this—even if it killed him to listen to the
Duchess go on and on about him being excited
to be a bachelor again—as though he were
happy to be rid of Enora. The thought sliced
into his heart. Nothing could be further from
the truth. "We need to know what to do next."

Bea hesitated. And then she continued reading.

Ladies, it's time to get out there. You never
know where the Duke is likely to pop up next.
And it appears he hasn't set his sights on anyone in particular. Well…

He might have spent most of his time tour-
ing the gallery with Princess Beatrix on his
arm. But was this the spark of a new romance?
Or is it more likely it was just two old friends
reconnecting?

Beatrix squealed.

"What's wrong?" He almost regretted asking the question because he didn't want anything else to be wrong. He was so over this whole fiasco.

"Nothing." At last the dark clouds had parted and the sunshine of her smile beamed through. "It's working."

"It is?"

She nodded and then held her phone out for him to see. There was a photo of her and Rez. This time he wasn't frowning and neither was she. Instead they appeared to be discussing a piece of art. It certainly wasn't a scandalous photo, nor was it one of contention. It was a rather neutral photo.

"We have to avoid this going forward," Bea said.

Once more he was confused. That seemed to happen a lot when he was talking to her. "Avoid what? I thought the point of this whole plan was for us to be seen together."

"It is. But this photo is blah. There's nothing here for people to gossip about."

"That's a good thing." People gossiped about the royal family way too much in his opinion.

"Not in this case. Remember, we're supposed to divert attention away from Istvan.

However, when I look at this post, most of it is about you." When he arched a brow, she said, "And me. Either way. The more they talk about us, the less they speculate about Istvan's relationship."

"Is there anything else?" He might as well know what was being said about him.

"Not really."

Will there or won't there be a royal wedding? This royal follower would love to know the answer. I'm not even sure whether or not I'm rooting for Prince Istvan and Indigo. Instead of palace statements, this royal follower would rather hear directly from the couple in question because I have questions, many of them.

In the meantime, at least we have the dashing Duke of Kaspar to distract us and tease us as he picks a new duchess. Who shall it be?

Until next time...xox

His hands clenched. His private life wasn't one for public speculation. The truth of the matter was that he was quickly coming to the conclusion that he did need to marry. Evi deserved a loving mother. But he had no idea how to accomplish this when his heart wasn't into the task. It wasn't like he could just take out an advertisement on the internet. Or could he?

As soon as the crazy idea came to him, he dismissed it. There would be no ads. But it might mean he had to pay more attention to the women he crossed paths with than he wanted to. It was the only way to find a suitable mother for Evi.

He wasn't planning to jump into marriage right away. It would take some time to find the right person—someone who loved Evi as much as he did.

She had to keep it together.

Beatrix had never been so happy for the interruption of a *Duchess Tales* post because it diverted Rez's attention away from her being upset over seeing him with his baby in his arms. But why had it upset her so much?

Sure there was the fact that she couldn't have her own children, but she'd made her peace with that. Her life was good the way it was. She had her life of service—of giving back to the people of Rydiania. And her obligations kept her busy every day. She didn't have room in her life for anything else—certainly not a husband and baby.

Not wanting to think about babies and her solitary life any longer, she said, "Even though our plan is working. I don't have any plans for tomorrow."

"What do you mean?"

"There are no openings, no sporting events or society parties."

"Then we'll make our own event."

She thought he would have been relieved not to have to play pretend for one day. "What do you have in mind?"

"Let me give it some thought and I'll get back to you. I promise it won't involve me singing."

Guilt assailed her. She really did owe him an apology, even if she wasn't ready to discuss the reason for her mood. "I'm sorry about earlier. It wasn't your singing. I promise." And then realizing they were still standing by the doorway, she said, "Come. Sit down."

They moved to her sitting area that had two large white couches flanked by a couple of well-stuffed purple armchairs. She sat on a couch. He sat on one of the chairs.

"Then what had you so upset?" His gaze probed her.

She glanced away. "It was just…" She reached for the first thing that had bothered her that evening. "The way people are so eager to believe the lies about Indigo—to the point of attempting to vandalize her artwork. Who does something like that?"

He leaned back in the chair. The rigid line of his shoulders had eased and the twin lines between his brows had soothed. "I don't know. I was trying to figure that out myself. It's not common in Rydiania."

"That's what I was thinking. We don't have people acting up out in the streets. We don't have people throwing around angry words. So perhaps it's just one or two people trying to stir up trouble." This idea appealed to her so much more than the thought of her country devolving into turmoil.

"What have your parents said about the attempted vandalism?"

"I haven't told them. I thought they had enough to deal with at the moment and with my father's health not being the best, I didn't want to lay this on him."

Rez nodded in understanding. "If it is one or two people, how do you plan to handle it? Tell the Royal Police?"

She shook her head. "Not yet." She held up her finger to have him wait. She moved to the bedroom door and pushed it closed. Then she returned to her seat. "First, I'd like to find out if we really do have a spy in our midst."

His eyes widened. "You're planning to flush out the spy?"

"I am."

"This sounds like an awful idea."

"Why?" She sat up straight. "Would you say the same thing if my brother had suggested it?"

Rez opened his mouth to answer but then wordlessly pressed his lips back together.

"That's what I thought." She didn't like the way her brother and Rez always seemed to think she needed protecting. After the things she'd had to face, identifying a spy wouldn't be so hard.

"And how do you plan to go about this ruse to catch a spy?" He arched a brow as though challenging her to come up with a good idea.

Feeling the pressure, she said, "Give me a moment to think."

"I think you'll need longer than that to come up with a good plan."

She ignored his doubt. The plan had to include a tidbit of gossip that was so interesting the spy would be sure to report it back to *Duchess Tales*. It shouldn't be something about Rez. He seemed very unhappy about the talk of his private life—not that she could blame him.

And she was willing to put herself out there,

but she couldn't think of anything that would be interesting enough to make it to print on the Duchess blog.

This left Istvan and Indigo. The thought didn't sit well with her, but maybe the news didn't have to be anything bad. Maybe it could be some good news about the couple. Something to keep the naysayers in check. The more she thought about it, the more she liked the idea.

"Oh, no." Rez softly groaned. "That is not a good look."

"What look?" She didn't realize her thoughts had transferred to her face. The thought of him being able to read her thoughts totally unnerved her. Say it wasn't so.

"The look that says you came up with an idea. And I have a feeling I'm going to hate it."

It wasn't as bad as she'd thought. "*Hate* is such a strong word."

He frowned at her. "Just tell me what it is."

There was a part of her that wanted to keep him guessing, but this was a time-sensitive subject. "We need to share something that is big enough news to rate a post on the Duchess site, but something that is positive for the royal family."

He paused as though thinking it over. "It seems reasonable enough."

"We need to let it slip that Istvan and Indigo have eloped." The more she thought about it, the more she liked the idea.

"What? Do you really think that's a good idea considering the circumstances?"

She shrugged. "I don't see how it can hurt anyone when the truth comes out except the believability of the spy and *Duchess Tales*."

"Do you think you should run this past your parents?"

She shook her head. "I don't see the need. If there isn't a spy in the palace, then it's no big deal. Nothing will come of it. *But* if there is one, this will give them away."

"How are you going to know who it is in the palace?"

"That part I haven't figured out. But at least we'll know if there is a leak. Because the only way they could have gotten the information was from us."

"And how do you plan to get this news out there?"

"I guess we'll need to make sure and talk about it around the staff."

"There's a lot of staff here. Like hundreds. How are you going to say this in front of all of them?"

"I don't think that's necessary. I think it's just the staff that are closest to the family we have to worry about." He didn't look convinced so she said, "Don't worry about it. I'll take care of it on my own."

His brows rose. "You're that determined to do this?"

"I am."

"I think it's a mistake."

"That much is apparent." She didn't like that he doubted her. Not at all. "So don't worry about it."

"And what about us…erm, our fake relationship?"

"We're still doing that too. What did you have in mind for tomorrow?"

He got to his feet. "I'll be in contact."

When he started for the door, she followed. "So that's it? You aren't going to tell me your plan?"

He hesitated. "I don't think so."

"Why not?"

"You seem to have enough on your mind at the moment. Let me take care of this. I'll let you know the plans in the morning." And with that he was out the door.

Beatrix was left staring at the open doorway and wondering what Rez was up to. Should she be worried?

As much as she wanted to figure out what Rez was up to, she didn't have the time. She needed to set to work on her own plan. She grabbed her phone and headed out the door.

CHAPTER NINE

His plan was in motion.

It was much more his speed.

The following day at noon, Rez pushed the baby stroller along the paved walkway through the park on the edge of the village. In his other hand, he held a picnic basket. He was curious to see what goodies the palace kitchen had packed for this outing.

With the sun shining brightly and a gentle breeze, it wasn't too hot, or too cold. This was the perfect day to be outdoors. He didn't like to keep Evi inside all day. He preferred for her to get some fresh air and explore the outdoors each day, weather permitting.

He searched for a spot to have a picnic. At last, he decided upon a grassy area at the top of a small hill. He pushed the stroller off into the grass. *Oh, yes, this would work just fine.* The green field was wide open with a few trees here and there. Best of all, it had a nice view of the rest of the park with a pond in the distance.

"What do you think, Evi?" He glanced down at his daughter. "Is this a good place for a picnic?"

"Looks good to me."

The unexpected answer startled him. He turned around to find Bea standing behind him. "I didn't hear you approach."

"Must be my stealthy skills." She smiled at him.

"You got here quickly."

"It's not far from the palace. And I might have been dropped off."

He arched his brow. "You couldn't walk that far?"

"I could have but I didn't want to be late. I had no idea what you had in mind."

"Would you mind helping me spread out the blanket?" He reached for the red plaid blanket draped over the top of the picnic basket.

As she helped spread out the blanket, she kept glancing around. "I don't see anyone."

He frowned. He didn't want this day to be about creating a buzz on the gossip sites. He just wanted all three of them to have a nice day. "Stop acting like you're expecting people to watch us."

"But I am."

"Just relax and pretend like you're having a good time."

She pursed her glossy lips as she looked at him. "Do you really think I have to pretend in order to have a good time?"

He shrugged. "This is all pretend... Isn't it?"

She didn't immediately reply. "Of course it is."

He finished straightening out the blanket. "Then smile and pretend like you're having a good time."

She smiled, but it didn't reach her eyes. It made him feel bad that she really did have to pretend to have a good time with him. He wanted the easy relationship back that they'd had all those years ago when they were kids. When they would play ball out in the rolling fields behind the palace grounds. When he knew that she was too young for him, but it didn't stop him from wanting to spend time around her because she was fun to be around.

It all seemed so long ago now. It was like he'd lived a couple of lifetimes between then and now. The life of a loving husband, who thought it was just the start of a happy married life. And then the life of a widower and single father, who had to fight through the darkness of grief in order to be a devoted father to his daughter.

And still he felt as though he was lacking in the parent department. He couldn't help but feel his daughter would benefit from having a strong, loving woman in her life. But the thought of remarrying—of putting his heart on the line again—had him hesitating. He couldn't risk going through another devastating loss.

"Can you hand me the basket?" Bea's voice drew him from his thoughts.

"Sure." He bent over and picked up the basket.

He turned to Bea. When she reached out, their fingers touched. Neither pulled away. The connection felt as though his body had been hit with a bolt of static electricity. It zipped up his arm to his chest. His heart felt as though it'd skipped a beat or two.

Was it just him? Or did Bea feel the arc between them? When his gaze met hers, his pulse increased. She'd felt it too.

The craziest desire came over him. His gaze lowered to Bea's glossy lips. He wondered what she'd do if he were to lean forward and press his mouth to hers. The impulse was too great to fight it.

As he leaned toward Bea, Evi started to fuss. The spell they'd been under had lifted as quickly as it'd started. Bea pulled her hand away from his. He immediately noticed the chill where her warm touch had just been.

Evi's fussing grew louder, distracting him from his thoughts of Bea. He leaned down and released the safety straps before lifting his daughter into his arms. She rubbed her eyes. Her rosy-red lips opened wide as she expelled a yawn.

With Evi in one arm, he rummaged through her diaper bag and pulled out some of her toys. He placed them on the blanket and then he set her down next to them.

He turned to Bea, who was unusually quiet as she removed the food from the basket. There was baby food for Evi as well as a large selection of cheeses from Brie to Camembert. A loaf of crusty bread and dipping sauces. Some meats were included, just perfect to make a savory sandwich. And then there was an array of colorful fruits. It all looked so tempting…but not as tempting as the woman seated next to him. His gaze strayed to her lush berry-red lips. They were just ripe for the picking.

As soon as the thought came to him, he glanced away. What was wrong with him? There was no way he was starting something with his best friend's sister, especially when he knew nothing would come of it. But it didn't stop him from wondering what it might be like to hold Bea in his arms.

For a while, they ate quietly. All the while he wondered what Bea was thinking. Was it possible she was having the same errant thoughts as him?

Bea glanced around as though checking to see if anyone was staring at them. "Did you contact someone in the press to let them know we'd be here?"

"No." She definitely wasn't on the same train of thought as him. He cleared his throat. "Didn't you say there was a spy in the palace? If so, wouldn't they know we were here?"

"Shh…" She glanced over at a young couple making their way along the sidewalk. Bea smiled at them. Once the couple had passed on by, she turned to him. "You have to be careful. You never know who's listening."

He was surprised by how seriously she was taking all of this spy stuff. It also made him wonder if she'd acted on her plan to ferret out the leak at the palace…if there was one.

"Did you work on flushing out the leak?"

She nodded. "I started last night."

"And how did you do this?" He wasn't sure he wanted to know the answer. He didn't like the thought of her doing anything the least bit dangerous.

"I had fake phone conversations."

It wasn't the answer he was expecting, but at least it seemed safe enough. "And who were these conversations with?"

"Istvan. During the conversation I learned he and Indigo eloped."

"Really?"

She smiled and nodded. "Now, we have to wait and see if it shows up on the *Duchess Tales* site today."

He had a hard time believing there was a spy in the palace. He knew the review process before being hired was extensive and a strong work history was a requirement. He knew this because he'd used a similar process for his country estate. If he was going to share his home with strangers, he wanted to protect his family's privacy.

"And has anything appeared on the site?" He hoped the answer was no because the royal family already had enough things to worry about.

"Not the last time I checked." She reached for her phone and pulled up the site. She gasped.

Concern filled him. "What is it?"

"It's there. The story of my brother and Indigo eloping." She looked at him. "There's definitely a spy in the palace."

When she went to stand up, he reached out for her hand. Immediately the feel of her soft, warm skin sent a jolt through his body. His thumb, as of its own volition, stroked the back of her hand.

It was a simple touch. It shouldn't have meant anything. And yet it was as though the touch had awakened a part of him that had been dormant for so long.

When his gaze met Bea's, he didn't see his childhood friend. Instead, he saw the grown woman she'd become. He noticed how her eyes had become windows to her soul. He found himself drowning in their blue depths. Her face had thinned out, revealing her high cheekbones. And then there were her full lips that appeared so perfect for kissing.

Bea stood, jarring him from his thoughts.

"Where are you going?" His voice came out deeper than normal.

"I have to inform the King. We have to find out who the spy is and get rid of them."

"Wait. Let's think about this." When she settled back on her spot on the blanket, he regretfully let go of their connection.

"Think about what? This is big. We can't have a spy within the palace."

"But what if you did leave them there?"

"Why?" She frowned at him.

"In order to funnel misinformation directly to the *Duchess Tales*. I mean you have a direct pipeline now to the biggest gossip site in all of Rydiania. Why would you cut that off when you need to get stories to the site as quickly as possible?"

She paused as though giving his idea some legitimate consideration. Her brows drew together. Her tempting lips pursed and every time he looked at them, he could feel a renewed desire swelling within him to pull her close and feel her lips beneath his.

"Maybe you're right." Her voice startled him from his thoughts. "In fact, the more I think about it, the more I like the idea. Rez, did you hear me?"

"Um...yes."

She studied him. "You were frowning at me like I'd done something to bother you—like you were doing at the polo match. What's wrong?"

He shook his head and replaced his supposed frown with a smile, hoping to ease her worry. "Nothing at all."

"You know, you were really good at the polo match. You looked like you were enjoying yourself. You should consider rejoining the team."

The thought was tempting. He had enjoyed

himself out there in the sunshine and on the back of his favorite polo pony. And as much as he'd enjoyed it, he knew he didn't even deserve that bit of happiness.

He shook his head. "I can't."

"Can't? Why not?" Her gaze searched his.

He lowered his gaze to the blanket. "It doesn't matter."

"Of course it matters. Especially if it's the reason you've been isolating yourself."

He knew Bea well enough to know she wasn't going to give up until she learned the truth. It was a story he hadn't been willing to share with anyone.

He could feel her expectant gaze on him. He turned to Evi. He picked her up and gave her a toy. All the while, Bea was quiet as she waited for him to answer her.

"It's a nice day." He hoped she'd go with it. "And the food was delicious."

"You aren't getting off that easily. I know you've been through a lot and I want to understand."

He turned to her and saw the caring look in her eyes. Maybe if he told her, she would understand why he didn't deserve to resume his former life—not with his wife no longer alive. But did he have the strength to voice the painful words?

He glanced down at Evi, who had fallen asleep in his arms. He cleared his throat as he struggled to find a starting point. "That day I was supposed to meet Enora and Evi for lunch. You have no idea how much I wish I could redo things that day."

Bea squeezed his arm. He found strength in her touch. He knew it was time he vocalized what had happened that day.

"Enora called me that morning and we made plans to meet up in town for lunch. Evi had been a couple of months old and Enora was anxious to get out of the house." He remembered that day vividly. "Only when it was finally time for lunch, I was tied up with a conference call." Back then he was a full partner at a big law firm. "And I...I put my work over my family."

"Is that why you haven't been back to work since then?"

He nodded. Just the thought of returning to the office reminded him of the worst day of his life. He didn't know if he'd ever be able to return to the same office. Not that he had to work. He'd inherited a fortune from his grandmother's estate. But as he was quickly finding, he had too much time on his hands.

"That day I decided to continue my business call instead of meeting my wife and daughter. If…If I had kept my word to Enora, none of that would have happened."

Bea squeezed his arm again and then slid her hand down to interlock her fingers with his. "You don't know that."

"I do know it. She wouldn't have been crossing the road at that moment. If it wasn't for your brother seeing her, I would have lost both her and Evi." The painful memories made the breath catch in his chest. It took him a moment to be able to speak again. "If your brother hadn't pushed the stroller out of the way…"

He couldn't finish the words. He couldn't think about losing Evi too. When he'd received the call at the office, he felt as though the bottom had totally dropped out of his world.

"I'd raced to the hospital. Enora had come to and I'd spoken to her very briefly before she'd gone into emergency surgery. She'd fought to live, but…" The memory tore at his heart. When he spoke again, it was barely more than a whisper. "She didn't make it."

"That's why you agreed to this crazy scheme to get the press's attention away from Istvan and Indigo?"

He nodded. "I owe your brother more than I can ever repay him."

"You do know he doesn't feel that way. He just wanted to help."

"I know. I couldn't imagine my life now if he hadn't stepped in. Your brother is my very best friend as far back as I can remember. But he shouldn't have had to do anything if I had been where I belonged. Enora's death is on me."

"No, it isn't. It's the fault of that twenty-year-old kid who was speeding and hit her. None of it is on you. And if Enora was here now, she would tell you that."

He wanted to believe Bea. He really did. But there was still a nagging voice at the back of his mind that said if only... Evi would still have her mother.

"I'm so sorry for all you've been going through." Bea's voice interrupted his thoughts. "I should have tried to see you more. I just didn't know what to say or what to do. I'm sorry for that. I wasn't a good friend." She lowered her head. "I'll do better."

He reached out and placed a finger beneath her chin, lifting until their gazes met. "You are an amazing friend. I don't know if I could have ever left my home and reentered society if you weren't by my side. You've made it a lot easier for me. How did I get so lucky to have you in my life?"

She smiled at him. "I'm the lucky one."

Is that what she really thought? She enjoyed having him in her life? His heart beat faster.

It felt like forever since an adult enjoyed his company. His gaze lowered to her glossy lips that shimmered in the sunlight. He should look away but he couldn't.

In that moment he needed a physical connection to remind him that he was more than a shell of a human who'd gotten lost in his grief. Bea was like a beacon, guiding him back to the land of the living. He was attracted to her in a way he'd never been drawn to anyone before.

Without thinking about where they were or who might see them, he leaned toward her. His heart beat so loud that it echoed in his ears. He pressed his mouth to hers.

Bea's lips were soft and smooth. His kiss was slow and gentle. He didn't want to rush this tantalizing exploration. He longed to savor this special moment as long as Bea would allow.

As the blood quickly pulsed through his veins and his chest filled with a radiating warmth, he felt fully alive once more. Bea's kiss reminded him of all he'd been missing in life. And now he wanted this moment to go on and on.

Evi shifted in his arm, drawing him out of the spell he was under. He drew back from Bea. He was about to apologize for kissing her, but the words died in the back of his throat. The truth is that he wasn't sorry. Not one little bit.

In fact, he very much wanted to kiss her again. His fingers tingled with the need to reach out and draw her to him. Maybe it wasn't too late to revisit the kiss.

But was it the right thing to do for either of them? He inwardly groaned. In the past, he'd acted in the moment and dealt with the consequences later. Now that he was a father, he found himself thinking before acting.

Bea was saying something but he was so caught up in the push-pull of his thoughts that he couldn't hear her. Soon his desire to feel her lips pressed to his was winning the struggle. It wouldn't take much to lean over to her.

"I should go." Bea went to stand.

Rez reached out to her. At first, he went to touch her hand, but having second thoughts, he rested his hand on her lower arm. "Don't leave."

She pulled her arm away. "That shouldn't have happened."

"You're right." He'd crossed a line. "Can we write it off as us getting caught up in the moment?"

There had to be a way to get things back on track. Now that there was possibly a spy in the palace, he worried if Bea was left to her own devices that she'd get into trouble. He had to make sure that didn't happen.

She didn't respond.

"It was just a kiss," he said casually as though it was common for him to go around kissing all of the pretty ladies. "We were eventually supposed to do that for the cameras, right?" When she silently nodded, he continued. "Now we've gotten the awkwardness of the first kiss out of the way." Nothing about the kiss had felt awkward—not in the least. "And when we do it in front of the cameras, it'll seem natural."

Her hesitant gaze searched him. Did she believe the bit of fiction he'd concocted? He hoped so. He didn't want to delve into the real reason he'd kissed her.

"And that's the only reason you kissed me?"

"Yes." The lie came out a little too quickly.

Bea settled back on the blanket. She was unusually quiet. It made him wonder what she was thinking. He filled the awkward silence with casual conversation, hoping to draw her back out.

He turned to his daughter, who was now awake and ready to play. He situated her on the blanket with her pink bouncy ball. When she batted the ball away, he rolled it back to her. Evi laughed. The lyrical sound filled his heart with joy.

Evi batted her bouncy ball harder than she'd ever done before. She was getting strong. The ball bounced off the blanket before he could reach it. It continued its journey over the green grass as it continued to make its way downhill.

Evi's bottom lip began to quiver as she watched the ball roll away. He knew what was coming next, her wail of anger. His daughter was not afraid to voice her displeasure. When she was upset, everyone in the vicinity knew.

Before she could let out her first wail, he reached in the diaper bag and produced her favorite stuffed animal. It was a white bear with a pink bow and he'd learned quickly that they couldn't go anywhere without it. Not if he wanted his hearing intact when they returned.

He handed it to her. Evi batted it away. Her gaze strayed to the direction of the ball.

"Could you keep an eye on her?" he asked Bea as he got to his feet.

"What?" Bea's face filled with confusion. "Why?"

"I need to go get her ball." And then he took off with long strides to the bottom of the long sloping hillside.

Behind him he could hear Evi letting out another wail. He didn't have to pause because he immediately heard Bea speaking to his daughter in soft tones. His daughter's cries faded away.

A smile pulled at the corners of his lips. It was all he could do not to stop and look back. He could imagine Evi in Bea's arms. Bea would be totally animated and Evi would be enthralled with her. And he would no longer have to worry that Bea didn't like his child, which was silly. Of course she would like her. Who wouldn't? Evi was bright and fun. Her belly laughs were contagious.

And yet he noticed in the past how Bea had always made excuses not to hold Evi—always backed away. What had that been about? Although it didn't matter now. The problem was fixed because once Bea held Evi, she'd succumb to his daughter's charms.

Of course, he liked to think that Evi got her outgoing personality from him, but you couldn't tell that lately. Ever since Enora passed on, he hadn't been the least bit outgoing. Grief and guilt had entwined, making a super-strong rope that had held him hostage. But Bea with her sunny personality and prodding had freed him from his misery.

This was the first day where he could really feel the sun on his face. Today he didn't feel as though he were slogging through life just trying to make it to the end of the day. Today he was starting to feel like his old self.

And he had Bea and Evi to thank for helping him to make it through the clouds and to find the sun again. That's why he had such high hopes for the afternoon. If Bea and Evi hit it off, this could be the first of many afternoon outings. Who knew where they'd end up next. And the nice thing was that they didn't have to sneak around because this was exactly what Bea wanted—their relationship out in the open. And if the press made more of the relationship than there really was, then all the better.

At last he reached the ball and picked it up. When he turned around he expected to find Evi on Bea's lap as they played and talked. Instead he found Bea still in her same spot and Evi was across from her.

He didn't understand it. Evi was easy to

like. Why was Bea keeping her distance? Didn't she like children?

The last thought sent a worrisome chill through his body. The thought of Bea never bonding with his child had never crossed his mind. It left him with a fundamental disappointment.

As he trudged up the hill, he had to know why Bea would prefer leaning the whole way across the blanket to hand Evi her stuffed animal when she tossed it aside, instead of Bea moving closer to her or even picking her up. But when he reached the blanket, Evi whined. He checked the time. It was time for her afternoon snack. He reached for some food in a pocket of the diaper bag. And then he got an idea.

He turned to Bea. "Why don't you feed her?"

Immediately Bea began shaking her head. "I don't think so."

"It's okay. She'd like it and you'll get to know her better."

She waved off the bottle. "No. I...I can't."

Can't? What did that mean? "I'll show you."

Her gaze met his. Her eyes shimmered. Were those tears in her eyes? She glanced away. "I don't want to. I...I have to go."

Without waiting for a response, she got to her feet and walked away.

He turned and watched her walk away. She didn't so much as glance back. When Evi once more fussed for her food, he turned his attention to his daughter. All the while, he wondered what was going on with Bea. Why was she acting this way? It wasn't the first time. He recalled how Bea was with Evi in the nursery.

Bea really didn't like children. The acknowledgment hit him like a gut punch. And here he was thinking that Bea might be a loving mother to Evi. He had never been so wrong.

CHAPTER TEN

WHAT WAS WRONG with her?

Why had she kissed him back?

Beatrix walked as fast as she could to the palace. When her security detail offered to drive her, she waved them off. She needed the time alone in order to sort her thoughts.

She didn't believe Rez when he said he'd kissed her to get past the awkwardness. There had been more to that kiss than some random, meaningless act. It had been tender and moving. And yet it had been powerful and full of emotion.

But was that emotion linked to the memories of his wife? After all, he'd just confessed the most traumatic moment in his life. His thoughts and emotions had everything to do with Enora. He'd been caught up in the memories of his late wife when he'd kissed her. That's all it was. It wasn't about Beatrix. Not really.

It had been the unexpected kiss that had

her making a hasty exit because it couldn't be sweet, little Evi. She was such an adorable baby. Anyone would instantly fall in love with her.

Try as she might, Beatrix couldn't convince herself that it was solely the kiss that had her so upset. She just wasn't that good of a liar. The truth was the sweet baby scared her more than anything else in her life.

Evi reminded her of what she couldn't have—a baby of her own. Before Beatrix's medical crisis, she hadn't given much thought to having a family. She had been young and single. And so after the surgery it hadn't been a big stretch to convince herself that she was fine with not having her own family.

And yet she wouldn't let herself pick up the baby. She was afraid she would know exactly what she was missing by not being able to have children of her own. She was afraid the pain would be too much. She didn't want to get caught up in the grief again. She'd already mourned the children she would never have—the family she wouldn't have.

Instead she needed to stay focused on her life of service. It was a busy, demanding schedule. It would be enough.

It was time to end this fake relationship. She couldn't do it any longer. They'd have to come up with some other sort of diversion.

She stormed through the back doorway of the palace and nearly collided with some staff that she'd never seen before. They were carrying linens in the shade of purple that had been selected for the wedding. It appeared they were working on more wedding preparations. Now they needed the bride and groom to return.

As Beatrix headed for her room, she pulled out her phone. It was so much easier to focus on someone else's problems instead of her own. And so she began messaging her brother.

When are you coming home?

Why?

Because everyone has noticed your absence and the wedding isn't far off.

Can't you hold everyone off just a little longer?

I'll try. But hurry home.

I'm doing my best.

Let me know if there's anything I can do.

It was all she could ask of him. She entered her room. Her great big bed with its soft pillows called to her. She longed to pick up a book and get lost in the pages. And then she realized there was nothing keeping her from doing exactly that.

Her steps quickened as she moved toward the bed where her e-reader rested on the side table. She kicked off her shoes and dived into bed. The soft pillows hugged her like a long-lost friend. It was there she took her first easy breath. She leaned over and picked up the e-reader. If she had her way, she would stay here the rest of the day.

With the cover flipped open, she perused the list of titles. Although she normally read romance because of their happily-ever-afters, she wasn't in the mood for that this afternoon. Instead she selected a thriller. She hoped the high stakes of the story would distract her from the problems in her own life.

She opened the book and read the first page. By the time she reached the end, she had to reread it because her thoughts had strayed back to Rez with his penetrating gaze that made her feel like he could see straight through her. No man had ever gotten to her the way he had. He could make her heart race with just a glance.

And there was his adorable daughter with her contagious laughter and those darling dimples. She would be so easy to love.

Beatrix let out a frustrated sigh. She'd lost her place on the page...again.

Knock-knock.

She wanted to pretend she hadn't heard the door. There wasn't anyone she wanted to talk to at the moment. Maybe if she sat quietly for a moment longer, they would move on.

Knock-knock.

"Your Royal Highness."

She sighed. Duty spurred her into action. She set aside her e-reader and slid out of bed. In her bare feet, she silently padded over to the door. She swung it open to find one of the Queen's ladies-in-waiting.

"Your Highness." The young woman bowed. When she straightened, she said, "The Queen requests your presence in her office."

"Right now?" She really wasn't in the mood to deal with her mother. Their talks were never light-and-easy conversations. Instead they were usually about a problem and this time she was certain the subject would be about the wedding.

"Yes, ma'am. I'll let her know that you're on the way." The woman turned and walked away.

Beatrix noticed how the woman didn't even

wait for her to reply. It was automatically assumed that when the King or Queen wanted to see someone they wouldn't dare consider refusing to make an appearance. It was the story of Beatrix's life.

With a sigh, she closed the door. She moved to her bathroom to check her hair and makeup. Her mother would comment if she didn't look her best. With her long hair brushed down her back and her hair band adjusted, she took a moment to apply some facial powder and repair her eyeliner. With one last inspection, she returned to her bedroom and slipped on her shoes.

As she made her way to the first floor, she passed many palace workers. They were carrying chairs and other furniture as the palace was preparing for the wedding reception next week. Now they had to hope the bride and groom returned before the big day.

When she arrived at the Queen's office, she was requested to wait while Mrs. Moreau checked with the Queen to see if she was ready for her. It wasn't missed by Beatrix that most people didn't have to be announced when they wanted to see their parents, but life within the palace walls was quite different from other places. Rituals were what made the royal family unique. And her parents did their best to stick to the traditions handed down through the generations.

At least they would be alone for this meeting. She wasn't ready to deal with her sister or, worse, Rez. Hopefully this would be a short meeting.

A few moments later, she was ushered into her mother's office. Her mother appeared to be in a pleasant mood even though she wasn't smiling. The Queen wasn't one to go around smiling. Instead the frown lines were erased from her face. And her eyes had a happy sparkle to them.

Beatrix came to a stop in front of her mother's desk. "What's going on?"

The Queen signed a paper and then leaned back in her chair. She glanced up. "I wanted to discuss the arrangement you have with Rez."

Beatrix nodded. "I wanted to discuss that too."

Just then the door behind her opened. Beatrix's back teeth ground together. This wasn't the time for an interruption. She was just about to tell her mother that she was done acting like she was romantically involved with Rez. She just couldn't do it anymore.

Being around him—being around his daughter—it was opening up the door to things she thought she'd finally made peace with and she couldn't have him undoing all of that. Not a chance.

Beatrix clasped her hands together as she waited for the Queen's secretary to announce the reason for the interruption.

"I hope I'm not late." The all-too-familiar male voice came from behind her.

Rez. What was he doing here? She resisted the urge to turn around. She wasn't going to let his presence stop her from what she'd come here to do. This charade had gone on long enough. It was time to end things.

What was Bea doing here?

Rez came to a stop. When he'd called the Queen's personal secretary and requested this meeting, he'd expected it to be private. He'd intended for this to be a brief conversation, but with Bea here, it might change things, depending on what she had to say.

By his way of thinking, he'd be home by Evi's bedtime. And then his life would get back to normal. He paused as he tried to picture what normal would look like now that he'd gotten back out in society. In the process, he realized he would miss seeing his friends. He would miss riding his polo ponies. He would miss doing things that kept him from dwelling on the void in his life and his guilt over his part in Evi no longer having a mother.

He continued into the office. All the while, he attempted to conceal his surprise at finding Bea here. Her shoulders were rigid as she held her head high.

Her presence wouldn't stop him from saying what needed to be said. This charade had gone on long enough. He hated to admit it but if Istvan and Indigo weren't back by now with the wedding next week, there wasn't going to be a wedding.

Rez noticed how Bea didn't even bother to turn and face him. He had no idea what had gone so terribly wrong. The thought that it had something to do with his daughter made him even more certain it was time to end this charade and head home. How could she dislike Evi? The thought was unimaginable.

The Queen's attention turned to him. He obliged her with a quick bow. After all, even in the most strained of circumstances within the palace walls, formalities must be abided to. When he straightened, he was unable to tell if the Queen was in a good mood or not. The royal family were well-practiced in keeping their emotions masked from the world.

"I'm so glad you're both here. I have some

news." The Queen's gaze moved to him. "But first, Rez, did you have something to discuss?"

He wasn't sure what the news would be. Perhaps she was about to announce that their fake relationship had failed or, worse, that they'd been found out, especially now that they knew there was a spy in the palace.

The last thing he wanted the Queen to think was that he was running away from trouble. His pride refused to let that happen. He was no coward.

When he hesitated to answer the Queen, Bea turned to him with an expectant gaze. He swallowed hard. It was best to find out the latest development before he told them his decision. "It can wait."

"Very well." The Queen reached for a newspaper on the corner of her desk. "I have been given an advance copy of tomorrow's newspaper. And you'll both be pleased to know that your efforts have been noticed." She turned the paper around so they could see it before she placed it on the desk. "I'm very pleased that you've both taken this job so seriously."

When Bea stepped forward to peer at the paper, he couldn't help but do the same. What exactly was in the paper?

He lowered his head to take in a colorful photo of himself, Bea and Evi. They were sitting on the blanket at the park. How had the paparazzi gotten this photo? He hadn't noticed anyone close enough to get this shot. But then he realized that with the vast vegetation the paparazzi could have been quite a distance away and taken the photo with a high-powered telephoto lens without ever being noticed.

It was only then that he read the headline: *And Baby Makes Three...*

As he turned his attention back to the image, he couldn't help but think they looked like a cute family. Evi was playing with her pink ball. And Bea was smiling as she watched his daughter. Wait. What?

He leaned in closer for a better look. Yes, Bea was most definitely smiling. So what did that mean? Had he gotten it all wrong? He was so confused.

"As you can see," the Queen said, "the country is captivated with you two. There was only a brief mention of the wedding. And though that normally would be a problem, under the circumstances, it's a blessing. So I want to thank you both and ask that you keep up the good work for just a little longer." The Queen turned her attention back to him. "Now, would you like to say something?"

His mind raced. What should he do? The

truth of the matter was that he couldn't leave here until he understood what was going on with Bea. She was giving out conflicting signals and he didn't know what to believe.

"I just wanted to say that while I don't mind helping out, I hope Istvan and Indigo return soon. I don't know how long it will be until we are found out."

"I'd like to say something," Bea said. "This charade is too much to ask of us. It just can't go on."

The Queen nodded. "I understand the burden it puts on both of you. No one wants to court the paparazzi, but it won't be for much longer. I've just gotten off the phone with Istvan. They will be returning tomorrow."

Finally. The tightness in Rez's chest eased. The charade would soon be over. At last they could get on with their lives. Being a guest at the palace was nice but it definitely wasn't relaxing like his place.

His gaze moved to Bea. She was quiet but the rigid line of her shoulders had eased. She didn't have to say anything; it was apparent she was relieved not to have to force a fake relationship with him.

The knowledge knifed into him. The pain was swift and had him struggling for air. Not that many years ago, she'd had the biggest crush on him. He knew. Everyone knew.

And though he'd thought she was cute for a kid, he knew he was too old for her. He'd moved on with Enora. He thought that part of his life was over and he would grow old with Enora. How was he supposed to know just how wrong he'd end up being?

But something had happened with Bea during that time. She didn't like him any longer. But why? What had changed?

And then he realized that it was a stupid question. Everything had changed since those carefree days of their childhoods. He'd grown up and become a husband and then father. And now he was widower and single father.

As for Bea, well, she'd most definitely grown up with her curvy goodness and those full tempting lips. But there were deeper changes that had her putting up walls between them. He wanted to break through those barriers and understand what was truly going on with her.

"That's great." The happiness echoed in Bea's voice. "Does this mean they worked out everything?"

"I hope so," the Queen said. "We didn't talk long."

"So you won't need us any longer," Bea said.

"Actually, we need you and Rez all the more now. With your brother and Indigo returning, we need to keep the focus off of them. We don't want any cold feet."

"But, Mother…"

"We'd be happy to help out." The words were out of his mouth before he realized what he was agreeing to do. Because there was no guarantee once he found out what was going on with Bea that it would improve their relationship.

Bea turned to him with a deep, dark frown. "No, we wouldn't."

"I've had my office come up with some plans for you two." The Queen continued as though she hadn't overheard the disagreement between them. "And this evening you are both going to the theater in the city."

"Mother, this is too much." Bea crossed her arms as though she were drawing a line in the sand.

He was curious to see who would win this disagreement. He'd had his say; now he was stepping back and letting these two strong women work things out.

One way or the other, he would have an honest conversation with Bea. He would find out what was bothering her. And he wasn't leaving the palace until he knew exactly what was going on.

"Beatrix, I don't know why you're fighting me on this. I thought you were in agreement that we needed to do whatever was necessary to secure your brother's happiness."

"That was before." Bea pressed her lips together as though she hadn't meant to vocalize her thoughts.

The Queen's brows drew together. "Before what?"

Bea hesitated. "Before I knew it was going to take so long."

"If you're worried about your calendar, don't be. My staff has been coordinating with your staff. All of your obligations will be taken care of." As though the Queen felt confident she'd addressed her daughter's concerns, she turned to him. "The play is this evening at seven o'clock. It is a black-tie affair. I presume that won't be a problem."

"No, ma'am." He'd made sure to pack a lot of his formal wear. He had enough experience at the palace to come prepared.

"Good. Then I won't keep you two. You'll have to leave here shortly. I'll have the car waiting for you. Now go. We don't want you to be late." Bea paused as though considering the benefit of being late and then she shook her head. "Definitely don't be late. We want your photo taken as you're stepping out of the car—together."

The Queen lowered her head and pressed a button on her desk. As she read some paperwork on her desk, the double doors behind them opened. They had been dismissed.

Bea turned and took long, quick steps. The rigid line of her shoulders had returned. She didn't have to look at him for him to know she was furious that he'd agreed to continue with this fake relationship. He could handle her anger. What he couldn't handle was not knowing why she kept running hot and cold with him.

Why was Rez siding with the Queen?

Beatrix wasn't happy with either of them. And yet she couldn't deny that their plan was working. Going forward, she was going to have to be extra careful to keep her distance from Rez and his adorable daughter. Because in the end, she didn't want any of them to get hurt.

The more time they spent together, the more confusing things became for both of them. It was obvious that Rez was lonely and missed his wife.

Her thoughts spiraled back to the spontaneous kiss they'd shared. It hadn't been her that he had been kissing. He'd been kissing a ghost—the memory of a woman he was still in love with.

And Beatrix couldn't be some sort of consolation prize. When she was kissed, she wanted to know that in his mind and perhaps his heart that it was her he craved. She didn't think that would ever happen. It'd already been a year and Rez was no closer to moving on with his life.

She gave herself one last glance in the full-length mirror. The navy blue dress with a crystal-studded bodice fit her perfectly. It was the first time she'd worn the gown but it wouldn't be her last. Not only was it comfortable but it also flattered her figure, making her hips not look so large.

And though the dress fell below her knees, there was a slit that led high up to her thigh. When she walked, it gave a glimpse of her whole leg. Is that the reason she'd picked this dress? She told herself no but there was a part of her that wanted to show Rez what he'd missed by not waiting for her—for not picking her.

With a deep calming breath, she reached for her purse, slipped on a pair of glittery navy blue heels and then made her way out the door. With it being the summer, she wore only a sheer shawl over her bare shoulders.

Rez was waiting for her by the front door. He was propped against the wall as though he'd been waiting a while for her. When he spotted her, he straightened up. She noticed he didn't smile, not that she'd given him any reason to smile at her.

As she made her way down the last couple of steps, she felt his gaze on her. A warmth swirled in her chest and then rushed up her neck to settle in her cheeks.

When she reached his side, he leaned in close to her. His breath brushed across her neck, sending a shiver of awareness down her spine. "You look amazing."

"Thank you." Her voice came out deep and breathy.

His gaze met hers. "If you dressed to turn heads, it worked."

His compliment made her heart flutter. "Thank you."

He presented his arm to her. "Shall we?"

She placed her hand in the crook of his arm. "We shall."

The car ride into the city was quiet. She felt Rez looking at her a couple of times. It felt as though there was something he wanted to say but then he changed his mind. Was he planning to apologize for siding with her mother about continuing this charade? If so, it was too late now. All they could do was their best to keep the focus on them and protect the bride and groom, who'd already been through so much in the press.

As the Queen wanted, the paparazzi were in full force outside the Rydiania House of Fine Arts. It was the oldest and largest theater in all of Rydiania. The building was one of architectural history with large columns and lions at the base of the broad stone steps.

The car pulled up in front of a long red carpet that led up to the open doors of the theater. It would appear tonight was a who's who of Rydiania society.

Her door was opened and Beatrix stepped out to a reception of people calling out to her. As was her practice, she placed a well-rehearsed smile on her face and waved to no one in particular. She noticed that Rez gave her a moment alone in the spotlight.

And then he was there by her side. The crowd went crazy with them together. His hand came to rest on the small of her back. Heat emanated from his fingers and seeped through the delicate material of her dress and into her skin. It felt as though his hand was branding her as his. Her mouth grew dry and all she could think about was him touching her. A desire began to burn within her.

After what felt like a million flashes went off in her face, they made their way into the theater. Immediately they were approached by some people she knew; others she couldn't put a name to their faces. She bluffed her way through the whole thing.

Rez's hand returned to the small of her back. The touch was comforting in a way and in another way it stoked the embers of desire. The heat of each fingertip burned through the thin material of her dress. She couldn't help but wonder what would happen if she were to turn in to him. Would he claim her lips with his own? Would he draw her up close to him? Her heart raced at the thought.

She realized someone was speaking to her and she had absolutely no idea what they'd said. She smiled and nodded before her gaze flickered to Rez. He sent her a knowing smile. She glanced away as heat warmed her cheeks. There was no way he could know she was fantasizing about him. None whatsoever. If only she could move away from his touch, she could think clearly.

She did a lot of smiling and nodding instead of speaking. She didn't want anyone to know how distracted she was, especially by the man next to her. Why had she ever thought this fake relationship would be a good idea?

When at last they arrived at their private box, she turned to him. Perhaps she stopped and turned too quickly because she ran straight into his muscular chest that was much like a solid wall. With her palm pressed to his chest, it was as though the connection had short-circuited her mind. And she forgot what she'd been about to say.

When his gaze connected with hers, it felt as though he was actually seeing her and not a ghost from his past. Her heart fluttered in her chest. She should have moved, but her feet refused to cooperate.

His gaze lowered to her lips. She felt an immediate draw to him. It was so strong that it overrode her common sense. It blocked out all of the reasons that this shouldn't happen. And instead all she could think about was how much she longed to feel his kiss.

She didn't know if she moved first or if he had done it. Or maybe they both moved at the same time. There was a roar in her ears. She didn't know if it came from the crowd in the theater or whether it was the rush of blood in her veins. It didn't matter in that moment. The only thing that mattered was the touch of his mouth on hers.

She lifted up on her tiptoes. Her hands slid up over the hard plains of his chest and then wrapped around his neck. She drew him closer.

And then he was there. His soft lips pressing to hers. There was a hunger, a need in his kiss. She met him with a need of her own.

She felt as though she'd been waiting for this all of her life. She should pull away. But she didn't. She should end the most delicious kiss. But she didn't want to.

Instead she let herself lean into his embrace and she kissed him back like they were about to say goodbye for a very long time. She wanted this kiss to carry her through the inevitable lonely nights after he returned to his estate.

The music began to play, startling Beatrix from the spell that had come over her. She pulled away from Rez. What had she been thinking?

She couldn't blame it on their ruse because there weren't any cameras around to photograph them. There weren't any bystanders to take notice. This time it was just the two of them.

Her gaze met his. She couldn't read what he was thinking. It was as though he'd put up a wall between them.

She should say something, but what? *I'm*

sorry for kissing you. But she wasn't sorry. It answered an old question she'd had about what it would be like to find herself in his arms with his mouth pressed to hers. And the answer startled her.

No one had ever kissed her quite like him. She felt the seismic waves from his kiss clear down to her toes. And now she knew that one kiss would never be enough. Was she destined to go through life comparing Rez with the other men that would pass through her life?

"Shall we sit down?" He gestured for her to go first.

Without a word, she moved to her seat. It was so close to his that their shoulders brushed. At the same time they both reached for the armrest. They could have shared it, with her arm over his and her fingers entwined with his. It was, oh, so tempting, but she resisted.

She just hoped no one asked her about the play because she didn't think she would be able to concentrate on it with Rez so close. Was he as startled by the intensity of their kiss? Did he want it to happen again?

She'd never know the answer to those questions because there was no way she would ever broach the subject with him. It was best just to pretend it hadn't happened. Oh, yes, that was definitely the way to handle it, even if she couldn't stop reliving the moment.

CHAPTER ELEVEN

HE YEARNED FOR more of her.

More kisses. More touches. More everything that was Bea.

Rez had no idea what had happened during the play. He clapped at the appropriate times and he'd stood at the end while the actors took the stage. And yet he had no idea about the storyline or the ending.

His thoughts were consumed with the scorching kiss he'd shared with Bea. He knew she hadn't planned it because she'd been giving him the cold shoulder ever since their picnic.

He certainly hadn't intended to kiss her. She still owed him answers for the distance she put between herself and Evi. What was it all about?

There was one undeniable thing between them—chemistry. When they were in close proximity to each other it was palpable. The more time they spent together the stronger the attraction became.

On the ride back to the palace, he considered questioning her about the kiss, about Eve, about all of it, but it wasn't the right place. He didn't want their conversation to be overheard. After all, there was a spy afoot and who knew who it was. The very last thing he wanted was for their private business to be splashed across the internet for everyone to read.

He noticed she was even more quiet than normal. Had the kiss caught her off guard too? And where did they go from here?

If he was smart, he'd pack his things, scoop up Evi and head back to the country where he belonged, but his curiosity about this growing thing with Bea overrode all of his common sense.

After the car dropped them off at the palace, he followed Bea inside. Now was their chance to have a private conversation. But where? His room? Or hers?

Definitely hers. He didn't want them to be disturbed by Evi, who always seemed to sense when he was close by. She would put up a fuss until he picked her up. Sometimes she would need a bottle to soothe her. Other times, he would rock her to sleep just as Enora used to do.

They'd just reached the grand staircase when the King approached them. He was using a cane, something Rez hadn't noticed the King using at other times. Rez wondered if the King's symptoms were worse in the evening or if he was hiding the extent of his disease from others.

The King's face lit up when he saw them. "Don't tell the Queen but I was just on my way to the kitchen for a late-night snack."

"Father, all you had to do was ring for one of the staff," Bea said. "They would have brought you whatever you desired."

He leaned on his cane. "They also would report it back to your mother and you know how she and the doctors fuss over my diet."

Right after the diagnosis, Istvan had mentioned the King had been diagnosed with Parkinson's. It appeared the Queen was doing everything in her power to see that he lived a healthy lifestyle.

The King's gaze moved between the two of them. "Am I to assume the plan for you two to fake a relationship is still going on?"

Bea nodded. "We are just returning from the theater."

"How was it?"

When Bea hesitated, Rez spoke up. "It was a decent play. The audience enjoyed it so much that they gave the cast a standing ovation."

"That's good to hear. Would either of you care to join me in the kitchen?" His gaze moved between the two of them.

Bea yawned. "I think I'll just go to bed."

"And I should go tuck Evi in."

"Okay. Remember mum's the word." He headed for the kitchen.

Bea watched her father walk away. There was a guarded look on her face, but Rez couldn't make out whether it was worry or something else. "Is something wrong?"

She shook head. "It's just my father is changing. Ever since his diagnosis, he isn't so serious anymore. It's like he figured out what's important in life and he's not stressing the other stuff."

"I'm sorry to hear that he's sick."

She glanced at him. "I thought you knew."

He nodded. "Your brother mentioned it. I just never had a chance to tell you how bad I feel about the news."

"Thanks." She turned and headed up the stairs.

He followed close behind. When she turned in the direction of her room, he turned that way as well.

A few steps down her wing of the palace,

she stopped and turned to him. "What are you doing? Your room is in the other direction."

"I'm just seeing you to your door."

She arched a skeptical brow. "Is that all?"

He couldn't help but smile. "I don't know. What do you have in mind?"

"Absolutely nothing." Her cheeks pinkened before she turned away. "I can get to my room on my own."

Her words didn't dissuade him. He'd waited long enough to have this conversation. He continued to follow her, even though she'd quickened her steps.

At her doorway, she suddenly stopped and turned to him. He found himself coming up on his tiptoes in order to get stopped before he ran into her. Although he remembered what had happened the last time they'd run into each other, at the theater. The idea appealed to him. Except they needed to talk and clear some things up before he gave in to the temptation of her lips.

"This is my room," she said.

He took a step back. "So it is."

"You can go now."

"I don't think so. We need to talk."

Her eyes briefly widened. "If it's about what happened earlier—"

"It's not." But was that the truth? "Not really."

Confusion clouded her eyes. She opened her door and stepped inside. He wasn't sure if she was going to slam the door in his face or invite him inside. He surmised that he had a fifty-fifty chance.

Then to his relief, she swung the door wide open. "Come inside, if you must."

It wasn't the warm invitation he had hoped for but it was enough for now. He stepped through the doorway and pushed the door closed behind him.

Bea placed her purse on an end table before kicking off her heels. Then she turned to him. "What did you want to talk about?"

Where did he begin? He'd had his words sorted in the car but now that they were here—now that she was staring about him with those bottomless eyes he could feel himself getting distracted. His carefully chosen words utterly abandoned him.

In that moment, all he wanted to do was take her in his arms and kiss her again. Because one kiss would never be enough.

The thought startled him. Was that wrong of him? Was he betraying the memory of Enora?

He recalled his wife's last words to him before they'd rushed her off to emergency surgery. She'd told him that she loved him and she made him promise he would go on with his life. But it all seemed so unfair with him here with a chance to find happiness again, while Enora was gone from this world.

The thought cooled his heated blood. And once more he recalled why he'd come here with Bea. He struggled to find the words but slowly they were coming back to him.

He cleared his throat. "Why do you dislike Evi?"

"What?" Bea's mouth gaped for a moment before she pressed her lips together.

"Since she's been here, you've avoided her. When I've offered to let you hold her, you always find an excuse to not pick her up. I need to know what that's about. Don't you like children in general? Or is there something specific about Evi you don't care for?"

Bea shook her head. "It's not like that. I swear."

He wasn't sure what she was trying to tell him. He stepped closer. "Then what is it like?"

Her eyes reflected some deep emotion. Was it pain? Perhaps sadness? He wanted to comfort her, but he didn't know what to say until she opened up to him.

When she didn't say anything and instead

stood there silently with a look on her face that said something was terribly wrong, he led her over to one of the couches. When she sat down, he took a seat next to her. All the while he wondered what was upsetting her so much.

He wanted to prompt her to speak but he knew he couldn't rush this. Whatever was bothering her would have to come out in her time, not his. The silence between them stretched on.

She turned to him. "It's not your daughter. I swear. She's so adorable with those chubby cheeks and her little laugh. Who couldn't fall in love with her?"

"I know. Every time I think that I'm not good at being a single parent, she has me striving to try harder—to be better."

Bea's gaze met his. "I think you're doing a great job."

"Why do you say that?"

"Because your little girl is so happy. You can tell just by looking at her that she's loved and she knows it."

He wanted to believe her, but there was this part of him that still thought Evi would be so much better off with a loving mother— someone who knew what they were doing. He had no clue from day to day. He did his best to be a good parent, but most of the time he was just faking it.

"She makes it easy to love her," he said with utter sincerity.

"I always thought some day when I got around to it that I'd have children." She picked a piece of fuzz from her dress.

"Did something happen to change that?"

She looked away at some faraway spot in the bedroom. "I have endometriosis."

He had a feeling he should know what that was, but he was at a loss. "Is it serious?"

She nodded. "When I first got the symptoms, they didn't think it was going to be too bad, just uncomfortable, but then things changed."

He wished he knew more about it so he was better able to offer her some comforting words. Not sure what to say, he reached out, placing his hand over hers and giving a squeeze.

"I ended up needing surgery and now I can't have children."

This information totally floored him. She'd always looked so healthy. "I'm so sorry."

She turned her head and looked at him. Tears shimmered in her eyes. "I thought I'd made peace with it, but then I saw you and Evi and I found myself realizing exactly what

I would be missing. I…" A tear splashed onto her cheek. "I…"

Her pain tore through him. He turned his body and drew her to him. Her head came to rest on his shoulder. He ran his hand over her hair while he absorbed what he'd learned.

He felt horrible that he'd accused Bea of not liking his daughter when all along she was dealing with a devastating diagnosis.

When she pulled back, her gaze met his. "I'm sorry you thought I didn't like Evi. She's so precious. I'm obviously still dealing with the fact that I'll never have a child of my own. The funny part is I was never one of those people who dreamed about having children. I didn't even know I wanted a baby until I couldn't have any."

His thumb swept away her tears. "It's still possible. There are other ways of having a family."

He couldn't even imagine how hard this must be for her. Sympathy welled up in him. He felt awful for jumping to the wrong conclusion. Now that he knew the truth, the wall between them had finally come down.

The truth was at last out there.

Beatrix hadn't intended to tell him her painful truth, but the kiss had changed everything. She realized how easy it would be for things to get serious. And it wouldn't be fair to him to let that happen without him knowing that she couldn't give him the family he deserved.

Now that it was all out there, she could breathe easier. At last, she wasn't holding in all of that painful information. And now Rez was looking at her differently. Sympathy shone in his eyes.

"Don't look at me like that." She glanced away.

"Like what?"

"Like you feel sorry for me."

"But I do feel bad." Honesty rang out in his voice. "You didn't ask for any of this. And it's not fair to you. But you could adopt."

Maybe. But there was no guarantee that a baby would be available. The wait could be long and the disappointment could be great. It was nothing she wanted to put Rez through after he'd experienced so much pain when he lost his wife.

"My life is fine the way it is." She hoped her voice sounded convincing.

"You mean you never intend to marry? Or have a family?" His gaze searched hers.

His questions poked in all the wrong spots, making her think about things she'd been avoiding up until then. She didn't want to contemplate them now. The answers were complicated. And she'd much rather concentrate on the here and now.

But as he continued to stare at her expectantly, she knew she had to say something. "Right now, I want to focus on my life as a working royal."

"And in the future will that be enough?"

She inwardly groaned. Why did he have to push this? She couldn't give him any answers because she hadn't figured them out for herself.

"I don't know." She barely hid the frustration in her voice. "I don't know what the future holds." She kept talking, hoping to stave off more questions. "I have a very busy life and I quite enjoy it. I was born into a life of service and I want to dedicate my life to being a working royal."

Rez looked at her differently. "You can't spend all of your time working."

What exactly did he mean? And then his gaze dipped to her mouth. Her heart began to thump-thump.

He leaned forward, pressing his lips to hers. Instead of their heated clench that had happened at the theater, this kiss was soft and gentle.

She enjoyed that he was taking things slow. It proved to her that even though life had thrown her some devastating blows that there was still goodness and gentleness around her. Her stress and worry faded away. She gave herself over to the moment. She returned his kiss with mounting desire. She turned her body to him and wrapped her arms around him, deepening the kiss.

He tasted sweet, like the champagne from the theater. With his arms around her, she forgot about her inability to have children, her feeling of inadequacy, her pain. In that moment, she was a woman that craved this incredibly sexy man, who held her undivided attention. It was as though she'd been waiting for this moment her entire life.

And then suddenly Rez pulled back. Disappointment assailed her. Her breathing was labored as her heart pounded in her chest. Beatrix lifted her head. Her gaze searched his darkened eyes for answers. Why had he pulled away from her? Didn't he desire her?

He continued to hold himself back. "Bea, is this what you want?"

How could he doubt her? Hadn't she shown him with her kiss how much she wanted him? But if he needed to hear the words, she would speak them.

"I want you very much. Do you know how long I've waited for this moment?"

"Waited?"

She nodded. "Don't you know how crazy I was about you when we were kids?"

"But you were too young back then."

"I'm not a kid anymore." She got to her feet and held her hand out to him. He placed his hand in hers as he got to his feet.

She led him over to the bed with way too many pillows. She had a feeling they would soon be heaped on the floor...along with their clothes. And then she turned to him. She lifted up on her tiptoes and pressed her lips to his. As they kissed, he reached behind her and worked the zipper of her dress downward.

CHAPTER TWELVE

IT HAD BEEN the most incredible night of her life.

The next morning Beatrix woke up alone. But it was all right because when Rez left before the sun was up, he'd awakened her with a kiss goodbye, which had started things again. It was like she couldn't get enough of him.

He was so gentle and more loving than she'd ever imagined. In the next moment he could be fiery and hot. And though she knew this time with Rez wasn't going to lead to a happily-ever-after, she intended to savor the moment while it lasted. She would make memories that would last her lifetime. Because as sure as the sun would come up the next day, she wouldn't forget her moment in his arms.

The only catch was reminding herself to keep things casual. She refused to allow her heart to become involved. It would lead to nothing but pain because she couldn't give

him the family he deserved. But she refused
to dwell on any of that now.

Her feet barely touched the floor that morning. She'd slept in late and missed breakfast.
Before one of the staff came to check on her,
she rushed through the shower. She wasn't
one of the royals that liked to be pampered.
She preferred to dress herself unless it was
for a special occasion like her brother's upcoming wedding.

And then she realized that Istvan and Indigo were returning today. She really hoped
they'd worked everything out and that the
wedding was back on track. Nothing would
make her happier.

She rushed to the door and then realized
she'd forgotten her phone in her purse from
last night. It was still on the end table next
to the couch. She unzipped the silver glittery clutch and retrieved her phone. When she
pressed the button, nothing happened. She
tried again. And again.

With a sigh, she conceded that the phone
was dead. It was getting older and it didn't
hold a charge like it used to. She moved to
the charging station next to her bed. Once it
was in position and the light on the charger
lit up, she headed out the door.

She wanted to go straight to Rez's room,

but she resisted the urge. She didn't want him to feel overwhelmed or anything. After all, it wasn't like they were in a relationship. Everything was new and had to be figured out.

She also had to get past her fear of getting close to Evi. Somehow she had to enjoy spending time with the little girl and not let herself dwell on not being able to have a baby of her own. Could she do it? She didn't know, but she really wanted to try.

She descended the grand staircase. With it being midmorning, she doubted anyone would be in the dining room. Still, she was hoping there would be some coffee and perhaps a croissant.

As she approached the private dining room, she heard voices. She stepped up to the doorway to find her brother and Indigo. And best of all they were smiling at each other.

"You're back!" Beatrix rushed toward her brother to give him a hug and then she turned to Indigo and hugged her.

"It's good to see you too." Indigo sent her a genuine smile that made her eyes twinkle.

"Does this mean the wedding is a go?" The breath hitched in her throat as she waited for the answer.

Istvan smiled as he wrapped his arm around his fiancée. "Yes, it does."

Beatrix expelled her pent-up breath. This was the best news she'd had in a long time. She had a feeling this was going to be a most excellent day. Now she had an excuse to be all smiley and no one would suspect that she'd spent the night in Rez's arms. She wasn't ready to share that bit of information with anyone.

"I'm sorry I freaked out." Indigo's voice distracted Beatrix from her thoughts. "I just wasn't expecting the press to be so vicious."

"I understand," Beatrix said. "It's a lot to deal with, even if you've grown up around the paparazzi."

"We wanted to thank you," Istvan said. "You've really gone above and beyond to help us."

"What?" She wasn't sure what he was referring to. And then she realized the Queen must have told him about their plan to distract the press.

Before she could say anything, her brother moved to the table and retrieved the morning's newspaper. "You must not have seen this yet."

"Oh, did they put a photo of Rez and me at the theater?" If it was good enough, she might have her secretary track down a digital copy for her. It would be nice to have a photo of them as a reminder.

"You might say that." Her brother started to laugh.

What was so funny? Was her makeup messed up? Or worse, did she have a wardrobe malfunction that she'd been unaware of?

Her body tensed as her brother handed her the paper. Once more she'd made the front page just below the fold. The headline read: *A Steamy Scene...*

The image before her caught her utterly and completely off guard. There she was in Rez's arms. In the close-up of them, her lips were all over his, arms wrapped about each other as they shared a passionate kiss. There was definitely no faking the desire in that embrace.

Heat rushed from her chest to her face. It felt as though she'd been standing in front of a sunlamp for much too long. She would swear soon her hair would go up in a puff of smoke.

"Good morning." Rez sauntered into the room. As soon as he looked at her face, the smile fled his face. "What's wrong?"

She shoved the paper at him. If this is what their conservative print paper had published, she wasn't sure she wanted to know what *Duchess Tales* had said about the kiss.

"Let me borrow your phone." She held her hand out to Rez.

His brows scrunched together. "Where's yours?"

"Just let me have it." And then remembering her manners, she said, "Please."

Without another word, he produced his phone. She took it and quickly sought out the *Duchess Tales* site.

"Perhaps we should give them a moment," Indigo said.

"I was hoping to hear more about that photo," Istvan teased.

Beatrix glanced up to see Indigo elbow her brother before taking him by the arm and leading him from the room. On their way out, Indigo pulled the doors shut behind them.

Beatrix glanced back at the phone screen to see the post about them was at the top of the site. Her stomach balled up into a tight knot.

The title of the post read: *Burning Up with Desire...*

She exhaled a groan. This was so much worse than she'd been expecting. It was one thing when they were trying to put on a show for the paparazzi, it was quite another when the press caught a genuine moment of passion. She felt so exposed.

Rez moved to her side. "Surely it can't be worse than what's in the paper."

"It's so much worse." Her gaze settled on

a photo of them with her body leaning fully against him as her fingers combed through his thick dark hair. It looked like—well, it looked like they were one step away from making mad passionate love. And the fact they had didn't go unnoticed by her, but it wasn't anyone's business but theirs. "*Duchess Tales* posted a full-length photo of us. It's like…"

"Like what?"

"Like we're making love with our clothes on." She inwardly groaned again.

"It can't be that bad. Let me see."

She turned the phone so he could see the image. He gave up his denial. When she turned the phone back around, she couldn't take her gaze off the image. Was that the way she really looked in his arms? It's like she was totally oblivious to their surroundings—that nothing mattered but feeling his lips against hers.

Rez's voice drew her from her thoughts. "It really is that bad."

"This is terrible. Now everyone is going to know about us."

He turned to her. "Bea, everyone already knows about us. Remember? We've been putting on a show for the paparazzi."

"But it's different now." She lowered her voice. "You know, since we slept together."

A grin came over his face. "Yes, we did. Again and again and again."

"Rez!" Her face grew hot with embarrassment.

"Okay. So what does the post say?"

Fellow royal watchers, I have to admit that every now and then I get it wrong. This is one of those days. It appears two more royals are off the market. That's right. Love is in the summer air.

The Duke of Kaspar has been snatched up by none other than our Princess Beatrix. She stole him away before any of the rest of us had a chance. So sorry, dearies.

But how can anyone deny that passion? It makes me wonder just how long this affair has been going on.

Obviously this wasn't their first kiss. Ooh-la-la. #steamy

Beatrix stopped reading. Her gaze returned to the photo of them. There was a part of her that longed for this casual arrangement to be something real. The thought startled her. Was that really what she wanted?

"What else does it say?" Rez's voice interrupted her troubling thoughts.

She held the phone out to him. "You read it."

She didn't think she could continue. Her empty stomach felt nauseous. Their plan had taken on a life of its own and now she wasn't ready to deal with the consequences.

Rez cleared his throat and then proceeded to continue reading.

Does this now mean there will be two royal weddings this year? Or is the Duke just getting his feet wet, so to speak. Is the Princess just a fling for the newly minted bachelor? And does the Princess know this?

Rez stopped reading.

In that moment, she wished it was true about the two royal weddings. But she couldn't ask Rez to commit himself to someone who couldn't give him what came so easily to so many other women—giving birth to a child.

Maybe they could adopt, but she knew the wait lists were lengthy and the journey was challenging without any guarantee of a baby at the end of it all. Could she put herself through that? Could she ask Rez to go through it after all he'd already lost?

The answer was unequivocally no. He deserved a wife who wasn't damaged and could give him more children in a traditional manner.

Her gaze moved to him. She could see the frown on his face. Was that pity that shone in his eyes? Did he feel bad that she'd read too much into their night together?

He stepped closer. "Bea, stop it."

She blinked repeatedly, refusing to let him see how much the implications of the post had hurt her. "Stop what?"

"Believing those lies."

"I'm fine." It was a little white lie. The truth was that she was anything but fine. "Read what else it says."

"Not before I do this." He lowered his head and pressed his lips to hers.

Even though she knew her family could walk in on them at any moment, it didn't stop her from wrapping her arms around his neck and kissing him back. His kiss was like a balm upon her scarred heart.

And as much as she wanted to continue this, she knew if they kept this up they'd end up back in her bedroom for the rest of the day. And now with the bride and groom back in the palace, there were wedding preparations and a garden party to attend.

Rez glanced at his phone and then back at

her. "Are you sure you want me to keep reading?"

There was a push-pull struggle within her. She didn't want to give any more power to *Duchess Tales*, but there was a nagging curiosity to know what else was being said about her—about them. She knew nothing good would come of it, but she ended up nodding her head.

Rez hesitated before turning his attention back to the screen of his phone.

I told you this was going to be an interesting summer. I did not lie. Now on to the rumor of Prince Istvan eloping. I don't think he would do this. I don't think he'd shut out his family that he's always been so close to. However, if there wasn't an elopement, then perhaps he'll come to his senses and return to his position as the heir to the throne. And he'd once more be on the market for a princess. I know you ladies would be lining up. Me included.

And don't give up on the Duke of Kaspar. This thing with the Princess might be fleeting at best. Rumor has it that she doesn't want to get married or have a family. But who wouldn't want to marry that sexy duke? Sigh.

That's all I have for now. I must run. Things

are changing within the palace walls quickly. I'll let you know the latest as soon as I learn the truth.

Take care, my lovely royal followers. Until next time...xox

Beatrix couldn't help but wonder if the Duchess's prediction was true. Would this thing with Rez be fleeting? Did she want it to be?

After all, she wasn't in the market for a serious relationship. At least she hadn't been. Now she didn't know what she wanted.

"Stop." Rez's firm voice drew her from her thoughts.

"What? I'm fine."

"No, you're worrying about that nonsense on the internet. And she knows absolutely nothing. Do you hear me? Nothing about us."

"But we still have a spy in the palace."

"Yes, you do. Are you ready to alert the King and Queen?"

"Alert us about what?" The King stood in the now-open doorway with the Queen next to him. His gaze moved between both of them.

Beatrix was actually grateful for the distraction. She didn't want to explain the photograph in the paper. Would they really believe it was all playacting and that they knew the paparazzi were there all along?

"You should close the door," Rez said. Once they had privacy, he said, "We believe there's a spy in the palace. Actually, it was Bea...Beatrix that figured it out."

Together they went on to explain it all to the King and Queen. Her parents were floored they had a spy among them. The King insisted he would set his best security men on figuring out who it was and prosecuting them because spying on the King and his family could rank right up there with treason. More investigating would have to be done. The King was already on the phone.

"Well, now that the nasty business has been taken care of," the Queen said, "you two need to get ready for the garden party we're having for Istvan and Indigo."

"I don't know, Mother." The thought of putting herself back out there in front of the public didn't appeal to her. Not now that the headlines were homing in on the truth.

"If you're worried about the press, don't be," the Queen said. "We have arrangements with the *Rydiania Press* to handle the party. No other paparazzi will be in attendance."

"I need to go meet with security." The King exited the room.

"I'll see you both shortly." The Queen followed the King out the door.

Beatrix couldn't believe what had just happened. Her mother hadn't interrogated her about the photo. She hadn't even admonished them about their obvious public display of affection, which most certainly went against protocol.

Beatrix turned to Rez. "Did that just happen?"

"What?" His brows were drawn together in confusion. "You mean talking to your parents?"

"I mean my mother not lecturing us about how royals are to behave in public."

"Maybe she didn't see the photograph."

"Ha. She probably saw it long before anyone else. My mother stays on top of any news that affects the royal family because our reputation is the most important thing."

He stepped closer and rubbed her back. "Relax. Maybe there's just so much going on with the wedding and she's so happy that your brother is back that she forgot about it."

Beatrix shook her head. "My mother doesn't forget anything."

"You know her best, but I wouldn't worry about it. Now come with me." He took her hand and led her out into the hallway.

"But I didn't have a chance to eat."

"Don't worry. We'll have food sent to my suite."

"Your suite? What are we going to do there?" Some very naughty thoughts came to mind.

"We're going to reintroduce you to Evi." He stopped and turned to her. "I'm jumping ahead. First, I need to know if this is something you want."

After her confession of sorts last night, she felt so much better. It wasn't like she could avoid being around babies forever. Her friends were getting married now and soon there would be babies everywhere she looked.

And Evi was so adorable. Beatrix desperately wanted to set aside her own pain and disappointment in order to get to know her. But was it possible? She didn't know the answer, but she was willing to give it a try.

Her hesitant gaze met his. "I'm willing to give it a try, but just don't expect too much from me."

"I have no expectations, but I'm not worried. I think you two will hit it off."

Her gaze lowered to their linked hands. It was with the greatest regret that she said, "Maybe we shouldn't be holding hands in the palace."

His gaze followed hers to their clasped hands. "I suppose you're right."

Once he let go of her hand, she really regretted saying anything, even if it was for the best. Together they climbed the steps and headed for the nursery.

The nanny was there when they arrived. She turned from the crib and her mouth gaped. "Your Royal Highness." She bowed. "It's so nice to meet you."

"It's nice to meet you too."

They made some pleasantries and then the nanny let Rez know that Evi had just wakened from a nap and had her diaper changed. Rez assured the woman she could take a break and they'd look after the baby.

Once the nanny was gone, Rez called the kitchen and requested a couple of croissants and eggs with juice and coffee. There was something special about having a five-star kitchen at your beck and call. And their croissants were out of this world.

Beatrix made her way over to the crib, where Evi was holding herself up and grinning. "Hello, Evi. How are you?"

The girl's blue eyes stared up at her. They were the same shade as her father's. Evi continued to smile as she jumped. Losing her hold on the rail, she began to fall. Beatrix

reached for her but she was too late. Evi top-
pled back on her mattress.

"Oops. Are you okay?" Beatrix didn't know
why she'd asked Evi that question when she
knew there was no way the little girl could
answer her.

"Is everything okay?" Rez moved to her
side.

"Evi got to jumping and fell over. I think
she's all right."

The baby rolled herself over, crawled over
to the rail and stood back up. The smile returned to her face.

"Let's get you out of there." Beatrix reached
out and picked up his daughter.

She drew the little girl close, feeling her
weight in her arms. As Evi's head came to
rest on her chest, she breathed in Evi's baby
scent. It filled her with a deep longing to have
a child of her own—a child like Evi, who was
the sweetest baby.

Tears pricked the back of Beatrix's eyes but
she refused to give in to them. She wouldn't
fall apart. This moment wasn't about her, it
was about Evi and what a wonderful girl she
was.

And so they all settled on the floor and
rolled the pink ball around. It appeared to be
one of Evi's favorite toys. Beatrix found when

she focused on the baby and not her problems that she was able to really enjoy herself. But every now and then when she let her mind wander, she realized that she would never get to enjoy these moments with her own child and it saddened her. She didn't let on to Rez. She didn't want to ruin the moment.

CHAPTER THIRTEEN

THINGS WERE GOING surprisingly well.

For the past few days, Rez had spent most of his time with Bea. Things between her and Evi had totally changed. Bea let down her guard with the baby and was really able to enjoy herself. He was happy for both of them, but it reaffirmed his belief that he wasn't enough for Evi. He'd watched how Evi had responded so well to Bea. It was obvious: Evi needed a mother.

But he didn't have time to dwell on it because he had to escort Bea to the garden party without any untimely photos being taken. They somehow managed to keep their hands and lips off each other, though it was utter torture for him.

It wasn't until the night that they were able to make love again...and again.

The following day had been an outing to the park with Evi that went so much better. And when evening rolled around, there was a formal reception for the foreign dignitaries who had arrived for the wedding. There was a lot of handshaking and small talk. And when the party wrapped up, Rez had once again snuck into Bea's room. He knew he shouldn't get too used to this because when the wedding was over, he'd be returning to his country house.

Even though Bea's relationship had dramatically improved with his daughter, he remembered what she'd said about wanting to dedicate her life to being a working royal. Her words had been abundantly clear. And he found them most disappointing.

The next evening had been the wedding rehearsal and all had gone well. At last, the headlines in the paper were positive and the Kingdom appeared to be excited about the royal wedding.

As they were seated for dinner, Rez was placed at the opposite end of the table from Bea. He really missed having her close by. He found that once he let down his guard, she fit so easily into his life.

He glanced down the table to where Bea was conversing with both of her sisters. They were laughing about something and Bea looked as though she didn't have a care in the world. He knew that wasn't the truth. And if there was something he could do to help her with her medical problems, he would in a heartbeat.

Istvan lightly elbowed him. "What has you so distracted?" His gaze moved to the other end of the table. "Or should I say who has you distracted?"

Not willing to discuss Bea with her brother, Rez said, "So are you ready to walk down the aisle?"

"Yes. I've always been ready. But you don't get to change the subject so easily. What's up with you and Bea?"

He shrugged as he tried to find an appropriate answer. "Why do you think anything is up?"

"Because you haven't been able to take your eyes off my sister all evening. And I did see the photo in the paper."

"We were just putting on a show for the paparazzi." And somehow they'd gotten caught up in their own pretend relationship.

"That wasn't make-believe. It was a real kiss." Istvan arched a brow. "So what are your intentions with my sister?"

Intentions? Really? They were going to have that conversation. "I…I don't have any."

"I know I warned you away from her years ago, but that was different then. We were just kids back then and you were too old for her. But now is different."

What was Istvan trying to tell him? That he should start a real relationship with Bea? No. He couldn't. His thoughts drifted back to Enora and how she'd made him promise to go on with his life. But could he start all over again?

The thoughts weighed on him the rest of the evening until it was time for them to retire for the evening. After all, the next day was the wedding.

But he wasn't the least bit tired. His gaze strayed to Bea and he thought of their nightly rendezvous in her room. The thought definitely appealed to him.

As though she could read his thoughts, Bea leaned over and said ever so softly, "Shall we meet up in my room?"

The answer *yes* hovered on the tip of his tongue. After all, it wasn't like they hadn't made love before—all night long. But it was now becoming a habit and habits led to expectations. And he wasn't in a position to live up to Bea's expectations, was he?

He was utterly confused. "I need to spend some time with Evi."

"Oh. All right. I'll come with you." She fell

in step beside him. "I didn't get to see her earlier because she was napping."

He checked the time. "She should be up now. And I know she'll be happy to see you."

And just as he predicted, Evi was wide awake. The nanny was just about to give her a bottle.

"Could I do that?" Bea asked.

"Certainly." The nanny smiled at Bea as she stood up. "You'll want to sit in the rocker. Evi loves it."

Rez stood back as Bea took a seat. And then with the nanny's help, she held the baby. Evi started to fuss. She was hungry. But once the bottle was in her mouth, she quieted down.

The nanny excused herself, leaving the three of them alone. He couldn't help but notice how well Evi had taken to Bea. He couldn't blame his daughter. Bea was pretty special. She had this warmth about her that drew him to her.

"Why are you so quiet?" Bea said softly.

He glanced down at Evi, whose eyes were now closed. Every once in a while she sucked at the bottle before she would doze off once more. "I was just thinking about how good you are with her."

Bea shook her head. "I have no clue what I'm doing."

"Don't tell Evi that, she thinks you hung the moon."

"Beginner's luck." As her gaze lowered to Evi, a smile lifted her glossy lips.

She looked like a natural with Evi in her arms. In fact, if he didn't know better, he might have mistaken them for mother and daughter.

He couldn't take his gaze off the two of them. When Beatrix looked at Evi there was definitely love in her eyes. They could be the perfect family...

In that moment, he knew that's what he wanted. Evi would have a mother. And Bea would have the baby she longed for. Now could he convince Bea how good they were together?

It was the day of the royal wedding.

The palace was abuzz with staff hustling here and there.

Beatrix couldn't help but wonder which one of them was spying on them. She didn't like the thought of not feeling totally secure at home—of watching what she said for fear it would end up on *Duchess Tales*. The King had his security force working on it, but so far they hadn't come up with anything helpful.

For the past few days, *Duchess Tales* had

been running positive posts about the wedding. At last they'd laid off Indigo. Maybe they conceded that nothing they said would break up Istvan and Indigo.

Right now, she needed to go help the bride get ready for her big day. The thought of her brother marrying the love of his life brought a big smile to her face, but it quickly disappeared as an ominous feeling came over her. What if something went wrong on her brother's big day?

She gave herself a mental shake. It wasn't going to happen. The worst was behind them. She just had to relax and enjoy the day.

She headed out the door. She turned a corner and almost ran into Rez. She stopped in time and took a step back. "Hey. What are you doing?" Her gaze took in his casual attire. "And dressed like that."

"I'm off to meet your brother. And what's wrong with the way I'm dressed?"

"It looks like you're about to go riding instead of getting ready for the wedding."

"As a matter of fact, I am going for a ride."

Her mouth gaped. "Now?"

"Your brother insisted."

"Insisted?" That didn't sound good. Not good at all. "Is he having cold feet?"

"No. He's just bored of waiting around." Rez

reached out and rubbed her upper arm. "Hey, relax. Everything is going to go smoothly today."

"I hope so." She didn't know why she kept having this nagging feeling that something was going to go awry that day.

"Everything will be fine. I should get going. Your brother is waiting for me."

"Okay. Be careful. We don't need either one of you getting hurt."

His brows drew together. "You're really worried, aren't you?"

"I'm not worried." It was a lie and they both knew it. "I'll just breathe easier once we get them down the aisle."

He nodded. "I understand. It has been a journey not just for them but us too. We weren't exactly planning to portray a couple. But here we are and I have to say that it wasn't as bad as I had imagined."

"As bad?" She was about to let him have it when she saw the teasing smile playing on his lips. "I'll remember that."

He glanced around to make sure they were alone. Confident of their privacy, he leaned forward. "Remember this."

And then his lips pressed to hers. Her heart tripped over itself as it beat in triple time.

He made it so easy to forget her worries. She leaned into his arms, deepening the kiss.

She longed to take him back to her room and have her way with him. But before she could put her thought into action, Rez pulled back.

He smiled at her. "Now you have something to think about instead of worrying."

"You're a really good distraction."

"Thanks... I think."

Her gaze moved to his lips that were now smudged with her pink lip gloss. "You might want to clean off your mouth before you see my brother."

Rez ran his fingers over his lips. "Thanks."

As he walked away, she smiled. Maybe he had a point. She had to lighten up. It's just that she'd been so worried about this wedding for so long that it was hard for her to relax—to believe it was going to have a happy ending after all. But she was going to hang on to Rez's kiss and let herself enjoy the day. And it was to start with a mani-pedi appointment in a room on the first floor.

She moved to the front staircase and rushed down the steps. Her sandals were quiet as she made her way across the marble floor and down the hallway. She turned the corner and came to a stop when she found one of the staff standing outside the room where the bridal party was to meet.

What was he doing? He was standing there, not moving. Was he spying on them?

He turned and practically ran into her. In his hands was an empty tray. "Your Royal Highness." He bowed his head. "I'm sorry. I didn't see you."

"What were you doing?"

"I…I was delivering some fresh coffee. Do you, um, need something?"

She crossed her arms and frowned at him. He was acting very nervous. "I need to know why you were lurking in the hallway."

Just then Indigo stepped into the hallway. "Beatrix, there you are. We were wondering what was taking you so long." Her gaze moved to the young man, who gave them both a wide-eyed stare. "Aren't you supposed to get us some gelato?"

"Yes, ma'am." He was eager to escape.

Beatrix's gaze settled on her soon-to-be sister-in-law's smile. She looked so happy, like she had that long-ago morning when they'd been having their final dress fittings. It was reassuring.

"Gelato, huh? Is that good or bad?"

"Good. Very good." Indigo linked her arm with Beatrix's as they entered the room. "We decided to have some gelato with our mani-pedi. I hope you want some."

"Count me in on the sugar rush." She returned Indigo's smile. "Today is going to be a wonderful day."

"Yes, it is."

And yet there was this teeny-tiny niggling worry that something was going to go wrong today and she didn't have a clue what it might be. But for now, she focused on the happy moment.

CHAPTER FOURTEEN

SIX WHITE HORSES led the white carriage.

Thousands of people lined the streets, cheering as the royal carriage made its way from the palace to the nearby village. Beatrix watched out the back window of the dark sedan that escorted her to the church. Indigo waved like the Princess she was about to become.

At the church, the bride and her mother exited the carriage and climbed the steps. The bridal party gathered at the end of the cathedral. Up close, Beatrix noticed that the color had drained from Indigo's face. It was a lot having thousands of people and hundreds of cameras in your face. Not to mention that she was about to marry a prince that came with a very public life.

Beatrix moved to Indigo's side. She lowered her voice. "Are you okay?"

"I'd be lying if I said there wasn't a dozen butterflies fluttering in my stomach."

"It'll be fine. Just a little longer and it'll all be over."

Indigo nodded. "I know."

The music began to play. Everyone lined up as the doors opened. Beatrix looked at Indigo. "I'll meet you at the end of the aisle."

"I'll see you there."

When it was Beatrix's turn to walk down the aisle, her gaze moved to the end and connected with Rez. Her heart skipped a beat. He looked so dashing with his morning coat on.

Rez continued to stare back at her. Beatrix would swear she had some of Indigo's butterflies in her own stomach. As she continued to stare back at him, she was grateful she didn't trip over her own feet. After what felt like forever, she made it to the end of the aisle. She took her place and turned.

A collective gasp echoed through the cathedral as the bride made her way up the aisle in the most magnificent snow white full-length gown. Her arms were bare as the strapless bodice twinkled from all of the crystals.

The skirt floated around her as she made her way along the red runner with her mother by her side. Indigo wore her hair up with just a few wispy curls that softened her face. But it wasn't the dress that made her look so radiant. It was the big smile on her face that made her eyes sparkle. Every bride should be as happy as her.

As Beatrix focused on the bride, she noticed that some color had returned to Indigo's cheeks as she smiled at her husband-to-be. Beatrix glanced over at her brother. His full attention was on his bride. A smile lifted the corners of his lips too. Beatrix took her first easy breath. There had been nothing to worry about after all. It was all going to work out.

The ceremony went according to plan. Istvan and Indigo exchanged their vows. And as was royal custom, they did not kiss after the ceremony. It was saved for a more private moment. Beatrix couldn't help but feel the royals had it all wrong. The first kiss of a married couple was, oh, so important. They should be able to express their feelings in the moment. If this was her wedding, she'd be kissing Rez for all to see.

She halted her thoughts. Why was she envisioning Rez as the groom? They'd both agreed to keep what they had casual. It was what she wanted, wasn't it?

Her heart pounded at the thought. As much as she'd been fighting her feelings for him, they had grown a fake relationship into what felt like a real relationship. She'd come to care deeply for Rez. Dare she admit it? She loved him.

The realization was huge for her. Her pulse raced as she came to terms with this revelation. She glanced his way. Did he feel the same way for her? She turned away. What was she supposed to do now? Act as though nothing had changed?

As Rez escorted Beatrix down the aisle, he leaned over and whispered, "Why are you frowning?"

"I am?" She hadn't realized her thoughts had translated into her facial expression. "It's nothing."

"I don't believe you."

"Shh…"

At the church steps, Beatrix was drawn away from Rez by the Queen. They were taking the back way to the palace and waiting for the happy couple there. They ended up waiting quite a while as the wedding processional back to the palace was very slow moving as the Prince and Princess's carriage wound its way through many of the village streets.

Once the bride and groom arrived, the pace picked up as there was a receiving line and a formal dinner followed by a large party in the ballroom.

Every time Beatrix spotted Rez from across the room, he was talking to someone. And it wasn't until she was dancing with someone

else that Rez was alone. How could two people keep missing each other?

It was getting late into the evening when
Beatrix's feet started to ache and she needed
to cool off. She moved to the doors leading
to the balcony. She moved outside.

The sun had already set and the palace was
bathed in moonlight. It was a beautiful night
as the stars twinkled overhead like hundreds
of diamonds. There was only one thing that
would make it better—Rez.

"There you are," came a voice from behind
her.

She spun around to find Rez standing there.
"How did you do that?"

"What? Follow you out here?"

"No. I mean yes. It's just that I was thinking about you and suddenly you appear."

He approached her. "I hope that's a good
thing."

"It's a very good thing."

They moved over to the edge of the balcony and stared out over the spacious gardens
that were visible in the bright moonlight. It
was such a beautiful evening. A warm breeze
rushed over her skin. And she felt all of her
stress and worries carried away.

"You must be relieved now that the wedding is over." His voice was deep and soft.

"I definitely am. And they both look so happy."

Creak!

Beatrix turned and stared into the shadows. She didn't see anything move. "Did you hear that?"

"Hear what?"

"The sound of a door opening." She continued to stare into the dark, wondering if they had company.

Rez turned to check things out. "I don't see anyone. Maybe they glanced out here, saw the balcony was occupied and returned to the party."

"Maybe." She turned back to him. "What did you think of the wedding?"

"That you were incredibly beautiful."

Immediately heat rushed to her face. Even with being a princess, she wasn't good with compliments. "Thank you. But I meant about the bride and groom. They looked so happy, didn't they?"

"Yes, they were happy, but it was you who held my attention. You were radiant."

She couldn't help but wonder what had come over him. Maybe it was the moonlight; it took the edges off things and obscured the details. Did he really think this about her?

She wasn't tall and slender like her older

sister, Gisella. And she wasn't cute and stylish like her younger sister, Cecelia. Beatrix was more on the short and curvy side. But when she looked into Rez's eyes, she felt like the most beautiful woman in the world.

She glanced away. "You don't have to say that."

"I'm not just saying that. You're amazing. And it starts on the inside. You're so warm and kind. Evi is crazy about you. And that's why I wanted to talk to you tonight before we leave in the morning."

"You're leaving? So soon." She should have expected this but with everything that had been going on, she'd gotten caught up in the moment.

He nodded. "Yes. Evi has been off her schedule since we've been at the palace. It's time to get her home."

She struggled with the fact that this tryst that they'd been enjoying was quickly coming to an end. "I understand."

He took both of her hands into his. "I want you to come with us."

This was the last thing she expected him to say. "Are you serious?"

"I am." He stared into her eyes.

The idea was tempting—so very tempting. "I don't know if I can take the time off. My schedule is really full. But maybe in a few weeks I could visit."

He shook his head. "You're misunderstanding me. I want you to become my wife."

"What?" She couldn't have heard him correctly.

"Think about it. You and I, we're good together. I think that has been proven every night this week."

The heat in her face flared. "That's no reason to get married."

"And you're really good with Evi." He paused. His gaze searched hers. "She needs you. And you need her."

She couldn't argue his point about Evi. They had formed a close bond. Nothing could compare to rocking Evi to sleep. She could just sit and hold the baby for hours.

But there was something missing from his proposal. He'd said nothing about him needing her. There were no words of love and forever. It was like he was forming some sort of business arrangement.

She did love Rez with all of her heart. It wasn't hard to love him. He could be kind, gentle and thoughtful. All she had to do was watch him with Evi and it melted her heart.

However, a one-way love would never

work. It would never be strong enough to handle life's tribulations.

In the end, their marriage would crack and disintegrate. It wouldn't be just the two of them that got hurt. Evi would be a casualty of them making a bad decision for all of the right reasons. And that little girl had already lost one mother—she couldn't lose another. Beatrix felt this overwhelming urge to protect Evi at all costs—even at the expense of her own happiness.

Besides, Rez would eventually come to resent her for not being able to give him more of his own children. Tears pricked the backs of her eyes. And if they tried adoption and it didn't work out, he'd resent her even more. It was best he marry someone without complications—someone who could easily give him the family he deserved.

That acknowledgment sliced deep into her heart. Rez was the only man she'd ever truly loved—perhaps the only one she would love. It was with the heaviest heart that she realized she had to turn down his proposal. It's what was best for everyone.

"So what do you say?"

She pulled her hands free of his hold. She couldn't say the difficult words if he was holding on to her. To do the right thing, she had to stand on her own two feet. She steeled herself, hoping when she opened her mouth that she didn't dissolve into a sea of tears.

She drew in a deep breath, hoping it would calm her. And then she blew it out.

"No." There was a slight waver in her voice because turning him down was ripping her apart. "I can't marry you."

Just then there was a flash of light out of the corner of her eye. They weren't alone. Her heart stopped. Who was taking their photo? It had to be the royal photographer because phones had been banned from the reception. They were collected before entering the palace and would be returned at the end.

"Who's there?" Rez's voice was more like a growl.

He wasn't happy. She couldn't blame him. And for their private conversation to be overheard was dreadful. Seconds ticked by as they stared into the dark.

"I said, who's there?" Rez wore a fierce look on his face. He turned back to her. "Go inside where it's safe."

She wasn't going anywhere without him, but before she could utter her refusal, Rez moved to the far end of the balcony. With the light on his phone, he began searching for the person that had taken their photo.

All the while her heart beat hard in her chest. She followed him and joined the light on her phone with his.

"Go inside," he said.

"Not without you." Her tone was firm and resolute.

Together they searched around the furniture and the multitude of tall, bushy potted plants. They'd worked halfway across the balcony when there was a crash on the other side of the balcony. Rez took off. And then in the shadows she could make out a dark figure before the mystery person took off down the steps into the garden.

"Rez, be careful!" Her insides knotted up with worry.

Who was the person? Certainly not a guest or the photographer. They had an intruder—perhaps the spy. And now Rez was out there in the dark with him. Anything could happen now.

She thought of following them, but she would never be able to keep up in her high heels. Instead she rushed inside the palace. She skirted around the party and headed for the hallway. She contacted security and told them there was an intruder in the garden. And she made sure to warn them that Rez was out there. She didn't want them to mistake him for the intruder.

And then she started to pace. There was no way she could go back to the reception now. She didn't want to ruin things for her brother and Indigo. They deserved to have a reception undisturbed.

Instead she headed for the King's office. She'd noticed that her parents had slipped out of the reception quite early. They claimed that the partying was for the younger crowd. She knew that with her father's health in decline that he didn't do late nights any longer. But she wondered if he was still up. If he was, she wanted to update him.

When she reached the office, there was one lone light on and her father was behind his desk. When he heard her approach, he glanced up. "What are you doing here instead of at the party?"

"There's an intruder." And then she proceeded to tell him how she and Rez were out on the balcony getting a breath of fresh air—she left out the part about the marriage proposal—and how someone took their photo.

"You called security?" The King got to his feet.

"They're on it. I just hope Rez doesn't get hurt."

"Let's go to the security offices and wait for word."

Together they made their way through the quiet halls. All the while, she couldn't help but wonder how such a lovely day had come to such a troubled ending. And now Rez was in danger.

Her heart clenched. He just had to be all right. Even though he didn't feel the same way about her as she did him, she would always care about him.

He refused to stop.

Rez kept putting one foot in front of the other. As he ran through the darkened garden, the only thought on his mind was capturing the person who had intruded on a very private moment—the person who obviously didn't belong at the palace—where his baby daughter lay sleeping upstairs.

Rez would continue his pursuit until he caught the person. All of his morning runs were paying off. He was gaining on the shadow of a person.

They rounded corner after corner until the person made an attempt to run across a clearing at the side of the garden. In the wide-open space, Rez knew this was his chance to catch the darkened figure that was undoubtedly a man.

Rez gave it his all. He expanded his steps and pushed himself to go as fast as he could. One footfall after the next, he grew closer.

When he reached the point where he could reach out and touch the man, Rez threw himself at the man. They collided. Their bodies hit the ground with an *oomph.*

They rolled around and struggled. Punches were thrown. Rez didn't know how much time had passed when he had the man straddled on the ground. The fight was over. The man gave up.

In the distance, he spotted flashlights. "Over here!"

Palace security rushed toward him. Once the man was restrained, Rez stared into the man's face. He recognized him. He was one of the staff that had been helping with the wedding preparations.

"Are you the one that has been feeding information to *Duchess Tales*?"

The man stared at him with anger in his eyes, but he didn't say a word.

Rez wasn't going to leave it like this. He had to know if this man had been spying on them all of this time. "Search him."

The guards produced a small phone. On it

were messages between the man and whoever was behind the *Duchess Tales* persona. At last, the palace's spy had been caught and would undoubtedly be prosecuted for his crimes.

On the phone was a photo of him and Beatrix. The image of them together made him pause. He remembered that moment so vividly. He'd been so nervous when he'd proposed to her. His stomach had been tied up in knots. He'd been so certain it was the right thing to do for all of them. And all she had to do was say yes.

He'd struggled to get the words out, certain he'd make a mess of the whole thing. When he finally spoke the words without making a mistake, he'd been proud of himself. Then she'd turned him down. The rejection had been like a giant gut punch.

He hadn't realized until that moment how invested he was in the family he'd envisioned. In his mind, the three of them would have been so happy. Apparently Bea didn't feel the same way.

How had he read the signs so wrong? With the lingering kisses and the repeated lovemaking, he'd thought what they had was something they could build on. So when he'd proposed, he'd been expecting her to be enthusiastic about the idea of making a family with him. He'd never been so wrong in his life.

The memory of her rejection sliced through him like a rusty nail being pounded into his heart. Why had she said no? The question circled round in his mind with only one viable answer—she didn't feel the same way about him.

It had to be the answer because he'd seen her with Evi. There was love reflected in Bea's eyes when she held his daughter. The realization only made her rejection that much more painful.

What was he supposed to say to her now that she'd turned him down? There was nothing to say. Whatever it was they'd shared was over. The best thing he could do for both of them was for him to head home. The sooner, the better.

CHAPTER FIFTEEN

SHE FELT HORRIBLE.

Absolutely awful.

Beatrix told herself that she'd turned down Rez's marriage proposal for all of the right reasons, but it didn't make her feel any better.

A part of her wondered if she should have agreed to marry him. Maybe he would have grown to love her. But it was too big of a risk to take with her heart.

That morning she'd skipped breakfast with the whole family, including some wedding guests. When her mother had stopped by her room, she'd blamed it on a headache. At her mother's insistence, she'd said she would join them later.

As lunch approached, Beatrix was still in bed. She had no desire to leave her room and wear a fake smile. While she was happy for her brother and Indigo, she was miserable for herself.

She had passed up a chance to build a life

with the man she loved and help raise the most precious little girl. Who did something like that? So what if he didn't love her. They were compatible in other ways. That could be enough. Couldn't it?

She pulled a pillow over her head and yelled in frustration. It didn't seem like there was a right decision. No matter how she responded to his marriage proposal, someone was going to get hurt. At least this way it wasn't sweet Evi.

Knock-knock.

"Go away!" She didn't want to see anyone.

The door opened anyway and in walked her eldest sister, Gisella. Her eyes widened when she spotted Beatrix still in bed. She walked over and sat down on the bed.

"So what's going on?"

"I have a headache. Didn't Mother tell you?"

"She mentioned it but no one believes it."

"What's that supposed to mean?" Why wouldn't her family believe her? She really did have a headache as she came to terms with what had happened the night before.

"It means that something happened. First, Rez leaves unexpectedly last night."

Beatrix sat up straighter. "Rez is gone already?"

"Isn't that just what I said?"

"But why?"

"That's what I want to know. He's gone. And you won't get out of bed today. So what gives?"

She wasn't ready to talk about it. "It's nothing."

"If you think you can keep it a secret, it's too late. And though I make it a point not to believe those gossip sites, in this case they might be right."

"Right about what?"

Gisella gestured to Beatrix's phone on her bedside table. "You should see it for yourself."

She didn't want to see it, but she needed to know what was going on. She turned on her phone and went to the most prestigious gossip site in Rydiania, *Duchess Tales*.

She piled up her pillows and then pressed on the link.

A Happily-Ever-After!

Beatrix breathed a sigh of relief. There was a photo of the newly married Prince and Princess. That wasn't so bad. In fact as she read down over the post there wasn't one mean or spiteful thing said about her brother or his wife.

"This isn't so bad. In fact, it's a nice write-up for Istvan and Indigo."

"True. But keep scrolling."

Beatrix didn't want to but with her older sister sitting there watching her, she didn't have much of a choice. Her finger moved over the screen.

REJECTED!

Beatrix read the headline again. Beneath the all-caps headline was a photo of Rez and herself. They were standing out on the balcony. And then she realized this photo was taken last night when Rez had proposed to her.

She gasped. She felt so utterly exposed. This scurrilous rag had taken her most private— most painful—moment and publicized it without care of how the people in the picture might feel.

Royal watchers, I have the most amazing news for you. The Duke of Kaspar has been turned down by the Princess. Yes, you read that right. She turned down his marriage proposal. The poor Duke. He'll probably need a shoulder to lean on. I'll be the first to offer him my own.

She didn't doubt the Duchess would be first in line to comfort Rez. The thought of any woman coming to his aid had jealousy burning in the pit of her gut. Why, oh, why couldn't he have loved her in return?

But she supposed she shouldn't be surprised. When she was crazy about him as a kid, he hadn't even given her a second glance. Why should the passing of time have changed any of that? It obviously hadn't.

You might ask why the Princess would turn down the Duke's proposal. It was the same question I have. And I'm sorry to say I have no answer for you. Maybe she is hoping to marry someone of a higher stature. Or maybe she doesn't want a ready-made family. Either way, it opens up the field for the Duke to search for a new wife.

The heartless words dug at her heart. This Duchess person had absolutely no idea what they were talking about. None whatsoever. If they did, they would know that status meant nothing to Beatrix. Even if Rez wasn't titled, she would have fallen for his charming smile, his caring ways and the way she could talk to him about anything.

Beatrix almost closed the app before she read the final words, but she hesitated. It wasn't like the Duchess could hurt her any worse than she had already.

With a broken heart, the Duke has departed for the country. So it might be a while until we see him again. But keep reading, my lovely watchers, and I will share with you as soon as we have a Duke sighting. Until next time... Duchess xox

"That woman is horrible." Beatrix slammed her phone down on the end table. "I wish we knew who it was and how she gets her information."

"So it is true?"

"No, it's not." Her denial came out too quickly and too vehemently to be believed.

"Do you love him?" Gisella watched her carefully.

Beatrix wanted to deny her feelings for Rez. It would make things so much easier. And yet she heard herself admitting the truth. "Yes. But he doesn't love me."

"Why would he propose if he didn't love you?"

"Because he wants a mother for his daughter."

"He told you this?"

"No. But it's obvious. There was nothing

about love or romance in his proposal. It was more like a business arrangement. And as much as I love him, I know that a one-way love isn't enough to make a lasting marriage."

Gisella was quiet for a moment. "He might not have said the right words, but I think you might be wrong about how he feels about you."

Beatrix wanted her sister to be right, but she knew it was just wishful thinking on Gisella's part. "I don't think so."

"Maybe you should look at the photo of you two again. To me that looks like a man in love." And with that her sister got up and walked out of the room.

Beatrix reached for her phone. Her sister wasn't right, was she? Her fingers moved over the touch screen until the photo came up on the screen.

She turned her phone sideways to enlarge the photo. And then she expanded the photo, focusing on Rez's face. There was definitely emotion written all over his face. Was he in love with her? She had no idea. She just knew without love, she couldn't marry him.

He hadn't been to bed at all last night.

Rez had paced throughout his darkened country home most of the night, while outside a summer storm raged. Bolts of lightning had sliced through the inky-black sky. Thunder rattled the home to its foundation. It was as though nature had mirrored his emotions and they were on display for all of the world to witness.

He couldn't understand how everything had gone so wrong. It was Beatrix who had encouraged him to rejoin life. She had been so encouraging that he was able to move past his guilt and let down his guard.

He thought Beatrix was the perfect person to let into his life—into Evi's life. Was it possible he'd let himself get caught up in the fake relationship they'd portrayed for the world to see? Had he only seen what he'd wanted to in Beatrix's eyes?

He raked his fingers through his hair. Even though he was home again, he could find no peace. The questions had tormented him all night. And now in the light of day, he couldn't find any solace.

Maybe it was exhaustion that was making everything feel so much worse. The only sleep he'd gotten was after Evi had awakened in the night wanting a bottle. He'd rocked her back to sleep and he'd fallen asleep in the rocking chair for a couple of hours.

Buzz-buzz.

He didn't want to talk to anyone. He ignored the call. When the phone rang a few minutes later, he ignored it too. Whoever was at the other end of the phone didn't want any part of his foul mood.

And then a message beeped on his phone and showed on his digital watch. He glanced at his wrist. The message was from Istvan:

Answer the phone. Or I'm driving there.

Rez inwardly groaned. He knew his friend well enough to know it wasn't an empty threat. When his phone rang a third time, he expelled a heavy sigh but answered it.

"What?" He didn't bother with any pleasantries. Even if he wanted to, he didn't think he was capable of it.

"How are you?"

"Just great," he said sarcastically. "How do you think?"

"I take it you saw the photo on the internet."

"No." He could only guess that it was the photo from last night on the balcony. He wasn't looking. He was already miserable enough.

"Do you want me to drive out there so we can talk?"

"No." His answer was quick and emphatic. "Aren't you supposed to be off on your honeymoon?"

"We aren't leaving for a few days. Indigo wanted some time to get her mother situated in her new home here in Rydiania. So I have the time."

Rez didn't say anything. He knew the harder he pushed his friend away, the harder Istvan would push back. Some things didn't change over time.

"So you proposed?"

"Yes." Rez rolled his eyes. He didn't want to have this conversation.

"And she turned you down?"

"Obviously." He bit his tongue not to be sarcastic.

"What did you do wrong?"

That question caught him off guard. "Why do you think I did anything wrong?"

"Obviously if you'd have done it right, you wouldn't be a miserable grouch and my sister wouldn't be holed away in her room all morning."

"Really?" He didn't think it would have fazed her to that extent. He didn't know what to make of that information.

"I wouldn't lie about one of my sisters

being miserable. So now I have to figure out what you did."

"I didn't do anything except ask her to marry me and she turned me down."

"Did you have a ring?"

"Uh, no. I didn't have time to get one."

"So this was a spur-of-the-moment decision."

"Yes...um...no." He wasn't sure what he meant.

"Did you get down on one knee?"

"Is that a requirement?"

"Of course. Women love a show of romance." Istvan paused as though to let the thought sink in. "Did you tell her how much you love her?" When Rez didn't respond, Istvan asked, "You do love her, don't you?"

Did he love Bea? The answer was a quick and resounding yes. Despite all of the reasons he'd found to propose to Bea, the main reason he'd done it was because he loved her with all of his heart.

Admitting his feelings scared him. And yet as the silence stretched on between him and Istvan, he knew his friend wasn't going to drop the subject until he answered him.

Rez drew in a deep breath and released it. "Yes. I love her."

"Did you tell her?" Istvan asked again.

"No. I didn't." He held back the fact that he'd only now acknowledged the true depth of his feelings for Bea to himself.

"Let me tell you a secret. Love is the greatest risk but it has the biggest payoff. And my sister loves you. I think she's loved you since she was a kid."

"When you swore you'd beat me up if I even looked in her direction."

"That was different. She was a kid then. Now you're both grown up. And I think you love her too. Otherwise I don't think you would have pretended to have a relationship with her and then sneak into her room each night at the palace of all places."

"You knew?"

"Yep. Just be glad it wasn't my father who found out."

Rez was very grateful the King never caught them. He had a feeling if it had been the King they would have been married by now or else he'd been put in the ancient dungeon beneath the palace.

"You need to make this right with Beatrix."

Istvan was right. There was so much more they needed to say to each other. But would she give him another chance? He didn't know the answer, but he knew if he didn't put himself out there and take a risk, he would regret it for the rest of his life.

"I'm going to need your help." Rez had a plan in mind.

CHAPTER SIXTEEN

HE HADN'T CALLED.

And she didn't know what to say to him.

Beatrix couldn't believe her brother and sister-in-law had insisted she join them as well as the rest of the family for dinner in the village. The very last thing she wanted to do was to get dressed up and go out in public. She didn't want people pointing at her and talking about her. They had no idea what the real story was with her and Rez.

After she had spent most of her day in her room, the Queen had stopped to check on her. She let Beatrix know she was expected at dinner. When the Queen put it that way, there was no arguing.

With great reluctance, Beatrix showered and dressed in a midnight blue dress with a plunging neckline. The bodice shimmered while the skirt floated around her legs.

Her lady-in-waiting came and styled her hair. It was all pulled up with just a few curly wisps around her neck. On her ears she wore diamond studs and on her neck she wore a sapphire pendant.

She took time with her makeup. Cover-up hid the dark shadows under her eyes. And a few eye drops helped with the redness. By the time she finished with all of her makeup, she looked almost like herself. She just didn't feel like it.

When she made it downstairs to leave for the restaurant, she found no one there. Where was everyone? Was she late?

She checked the time. She was six minutes late. They couldn't have waited for her? It was tempting to just go upstairs and forget about dinner, but she didn't want to disappoint her brother. After all, he was still celebrating his marriage.

She stepped outside to find a car waiting for her. She climbed inside. The car ride was short as the village was right beyond the palace lands.

It pulled to a stop in front of the restaurant. The driver opened her door and she made her way to the restaurant. The maître d' opened the door for her. She stepped inside and was surprised to find the place empty. She didn't even spot a member of her family. What was going on?

In the background, the song "That's Amore" was playing. It gave the restaurant a cozy feel. As she stepped farther into the restaurant, she noticed the lights had been dimmed. On each of the dozens of tables were a hundred candles. The flames flickered, casting shadows on the walls.

There wasn't another soul in the room. She was alone. Her gaze came to rest on the table in the center of the dining room. It had a white linen tablecloth with a large crystal vase holding dozens of long-stemmed red roses.

Had she misunderstood her family when they told her about dinner? Was this supposed to be a romantic dinner for Istvan and Indigo? Was she supposed to be having dinner with her family at the palace?

She was about to retrace her steps before she ruined someone else's magical evening. A movement caught her attention. Out of the shadows stepped Rez. He was all done up in a dark suit and tie. He looked particularly charming. No, she took that back. He looked hot—sizzling hot.

She swallowed hard. "Rez, what's going on? Where is everybody?"

"All of the invited guests are here."

She glanced around. "But there's just you and me."

"That's right." He approached her. "Your brother helped me get you here so I could explain things."

Her spine stiffened. Her brother and her mother had colluded to get her to meet Rez. She wasn't so sure how she felt about that.

"I don't know what we have to talk about." Her protective walls went up.

"Lots." He stepped closer to her. "I really messed up last night."

It would have been the polite thing to disagree with him and assure him that his proposal was no big deal when in fact it was a *huge* deal. He'd irrevocably changed their relationship and even if they got past it, things between them would never be the same.

"And so you did all of this for me?" Her gaze moved to the candles and roses before returning to him.

"I did. Yesterday, I acted without thinking through everything."

What exactly was he saying? She thought back to the photo in the *Duchess Tales*. Was her sister's interpretation of the photo right? Did he love her? Her heartbeat sped up.

"And you've now thought things through?"

He nodded. "I have. Bea, if it wasn't for

you, I'd still be holed up in my house. I'd still be punishing myself for the accident. You helped me see that I can't go on blaming myself. It isn't fair to me and it isn't fair to Evi. I need to start over and I'd like to do it with you."

"I'm glad you got that figured out, but I don't know if I should be a part of it." It was killing her to say it, but she didn't want to be his good friend—she wanted so much more.

"Of course you should. We've known each other all of our lives. We have so many great memories. And I'd love the chance to make more of them with you." He paused. "Up until now, I've been afraid to face my feelings. After the accident, I swore I'd never let myself get too close to anyone because the risk of loss and pain were too great."

"And you've changed your mind?" The breath caught in her lungs as she waited for the answer.

"I have." He gazed deep into her eyes. "The truth is that it's impossible to hide from true love whether you're willing to admit it or not."

Was he saying he loved her? Her heart swelled with hope as she waited for him to say more.

"And to deny such a love is painful and haunting. I don't want to miss this chance to be happy with you and Evi. I don't want to live the rest of my life wondering what might have happened if I'd taken a risk."

Tears of joy blurred her vision. She blinked them away.

"What I'm stumbling all over myself to say is I love you, Beatrix. I don't know when it started. I just know that pretending to be your boyfriend made me realize what was right in front of me—the woman I'm meant to spend my life with."

Happy tears streaked down her cheeks. She didn't think she was ever going to hear those words from him. "I love you too."

He reached out and pulled her to him. His mouth claimed hers. Her heart pitter-pattered. This kiss… It felt so different… It was full of love. And she never wanted it to end.

Her arms slid up over his broad shoulders and wrapped around the back of his neck. Her body leaned into his. Her soft curves molded to his hard plains.

How did she get so lucky to have him in her life? She didn't know the answer, she just knew she'd found her very own prince charming. And she never wanted to let him go.

When he pulled back, he smiled at her. He reached in his pocket and withdrew a black velvet ring box. Her heart leaped into her throat.

He had given this proposal a lot more thought. He wasn't talking about a fleeting love, but one that would endure. As much as she wanted to let herself get lost in this moment, her fears about expanding their family came rushing forth.

She couldn't pretend that just because they loved each other that everything would work out. She might be a princess but she didn't believe in fairy tales.

She placed her hand on his, pausing him. Her gaze searched his. "Are you willing to accept that I can never carry your baby?"

He nodded. "I understand. The three of us is all I need."

"Maybe for now, but what about in the future? You're such a good and loving father. What if as Evi grows older, you want another baby? You'll resent me for keeping you from experiencing fatherhood again." Her heart ached at the thought of him resenting her.

He took her hands in his. "Expanding our family won't be a decision one of us makes alone. It would be something we decide together and then we'll sign up for adoption."

"But adoption isn't a guarantee. The wait lists are long and even if you get selected, the birth mother can change her mind. I don't want to put you through all of that."

"You wouldn't put me through anything. If that's what we choose to do, we'd do it together and we'd lean on each other through the entire journey."

Her gaze searched his. "You really mean it?"

"I do. I love you and I want to be your partner through it all—the good and the bad. As long as I have you and Evi, I'll be happy."

He was right. And perhaps one day they would explore those options. But right now, she had everything she would ever need to be happy.

"Okay. Proceed."

His smile returned. He got down on one knee and opened the ring box. "Princess Beatrix, you caught my attention as a kid and now I see you as the beautiful woman you are. I love you with all of my heart. I would be honored if you would agree to be my wife. Will you marry me?"

By now the happy tears were flooding down her face. "Yes. Yes, I will."

He withdrew the ring and she held out her hand. It had a slight tremble. She'd never been so excited about anything in her life. And then the ring slid on her finger as though it were made for her.

She lifted her hand and stared down at the diamond-encrusted platinum band with a large oval diamond. It sparkled in the candle-light.

Her gaze lifted to Rez. "I love it, but I love you more."

"I love you too." He leaned forward and kissed her again.

It was the first of a lifetime of kisses—a lifetime of love and devotion. She was the luckiest woman in the world.

"How long until *Duchess Tales* finds out about our engagement?" Beatrix's gaze returned to the ring.

"It doesn't matter to me. I want the whole world to know just how much I love you."

She turned to him. "The whole world, huh?"

"Uh-huh." He wrapped his arms around her waist, pulling her close. "I could shout it from the mountaintop if you'd like."

"I have something else in mind." She lifted up on her tiptoes, pressing her lips to his. She could get very used to this.

EPILOGUE

Four years later...

LIFE WAS FULL of twists and turns.

Beatrix never imagined she could be this happy. She glanced over her shoulder at her loving, adoring husband as he stood near the window of their country home. He'd taken the last week and a half off from his law firm to spend time with the family.

Since he'd returned to his legal work, he'd been careful not to work long hours. They'd both learned to value their family time. It was for that reason that she'd lightened the number of projects she sponsored. Because when Evi returned home from school, Beatrix wanted to be there to spend time with her.

At Rez's insistence, they'd renovated the entire estate making it their home. And lucky for them it had plenty of bedrooms because their families were constantly visiting. Everyone wanted to spend time with their sweet five-year-old daughter, Evi, whom Beatrix had officially adopted. Though she insisted on helping Evi to remember her birth mother through pictures and home movies.

And there was another reason their families were spending a lot of time at the country estate: Evi's new baby brother, Alexander.

Beatrix had never believed in miracles before but she did now. While they'd been on the waiting list to adopt, she'd gone back to her doctor. He'd insisted there was absolutely no way for her to carry a baby.

When she'd inquired about using a surrogate, they'd done tests. She didn't have many eggs. And so at her insistence and Rez's great hesitation, she'd started IVF treatments. And when the time was right, she had surgery for egg retrieval. None of the fertilized eggs had been viable.

While the doctor and Rez had wanted to call it quits, Beatrix insisted on doing another round. This time there were two viable fertilized eggs. They were fortunate to be put in contact with a surrogate, who was willing to have the two eggs implanted. One egg didn't survive but the other thrived.

She stared down at her ten-day-old son, who was asleep in her arms. Just then she felt her husband's hand on her shoulder. She leaned her head against his arm and then kissed the back of his hand.

"Our miracle baby is a good sleeper," she said.

"He's just like his father."

"He's a mini you." She gazed down at her son's full head of dark hair.

"I don't know. I think he has your nose and eyes."

"You do?" She peered at their son, trying to see herself in him. She didn't see it, but it didn't matter whom Alexander looked like. He totally had her wrapped around his tiny finger.

"Can I hold him?" Evi ran into the room. She stopped beside Beatrix and stared at her little brother. "Please."

Beatrix gazed up at Rez, wondering what he thought of their energetic daughter holding a newborn. Rez nodded his approval.

"You have to sit on the couch next to your mother." Rez patted a spot on the couch.

Evi scooted into the spot and held out her arms. Excitement shone in her eyes.

Beatrix stood and turned to Evi. "You have to be super careful with him and watch his head. It needs support."

"I will."

"He's very small and delicate." Beatrix

carefully positioned Alexander in his big sister's arms.

Evi sat very still. Beatrix wasn't even sure Evi was breathing as she stared down at Alexander.

"You're doing good," Beatrix said.

"He's so small. How will he do anything?"

"We'll do things for him until he grows up a little. As his big sister, you'll have lots of things to show him." Beatrix wrapped her arm around Rez and leaned into him. She'd never seen such a beautiful scene.

"I can show him how to play hide-and-seek. I get to hide and he has to find me. And I can show him the tree house."

"Slow down," Rez said. "He's got a lot of growing to do before he'll be ready for all of those things."

"Mind if we join you?" Beatrix's mother's voice came from behind her.

Beatrix turned to find her parents standing in the doorway.

"Grannie!" Evi's exuberant voice woke her brother.

Rez took the baby and rocked him back to sleep. "It's okay, buddy." He spoke in soft tones. "You'll get used to your sister's excitement."

Beatrix watched as Evi was enveloped in her mother's arms. Becoming a grandparent had really changed her mother. Beatrix never thought her rule-abiding, proper parents would become doting, laid-back grandparents.

As Evi chattered to her grandfather about her new tree house, Beatrix's mother made her way over to the baby. As Rez handed Alexander over to Beatrix's mother, there was a look of love that came over her face.

Beatrix leaned against her husband. Her head rested against his broad shoulders. "I don't think I've ever been so happy."

"Me either." He turned to her. "I love you, my princess."

"I love you too."

* * * * *

Look out for the next story in the Princesses of Rydiania trilogy Coming soon!

And if you enjoyed this story, check out these other great reads from Jennifer Faye

His Accidentally Pregnant Princess
Second Chance with the Bridesmaid
It Started with a Royal Kiss

Available now!